JAX

Ink-Fusion Book I

PENNY ANGLENE

To: Kristiann ~
Enjoy the "start"
of this Series ~

Penny
Anglene ~

COPYRIGHT

WARNING

This book may have triggers for some people due to violence, crude language, and sexual situations. If you have any of these this book may not be for you. Please, consider this warning before proceeding.

DEDICATION

I started reading romance at an early age of twelve. My mom was a loyal reader of Harlequin until the day she passed away in 2009. It's her love of reading that got me hooked on not only reading but also the inspiration that I always wanted to write my own romance novel one day. I finally did it. If it wasn't for years of watching her with a book in her hand, I don't know that I would have had the courage to do so. So, from the bottom of my heart, I want to not only thank her, but also let her know how very much I miss her. There isn't a day that goes by that you are not in my thoughts. I love you, Mom. Until I see you again.

This one's for you!!!!

PROLOGUE

RIA AND DEBBIE - AGE 15

I'm sitting on my bed, polishing my toenails a bright purple, just bored out of my mind. It's summer break from school and I've been out for a week. If this is what the summer is gonna be like, I'd rather be back there, so I can see everyone. I hear the phone ring downstairs and wait to see if someone answers it. It's stopped, so someone did.

"Ria, honey, phone," my mom bellows up the stairs.

"Okay, mom, I'm coming," I yell down. "Sheeeit," I mutter under my breath. *My nails are wet; they're going to get messed up*, I think to myself. I get up and hobble with my toes in the air, praying they don't get messed up. I get downstairs and mom gives me a kiss on the forehead.

"It's Debbie," she says.

"Thanks, Mom."

I pick up the phone. "Hey, Debbie, whatcha doing?" I ask with a chuckle.

1

"Not a thing, want to go and walk the trails today so I can get out of this madhouse? The guys are in and driving me nuts. I need to get away for a few hours. I am bored outta my mind," she mutters loudly. I hear her brothers giving her crap in the background.

I snicker and tell her, "Yeah, let's do that. I'm bored too."

We agree to meet up in an hour out by the state park. I go back and let my mom know what we're doing and where we're going. She lets me know she will drop me off out there and will pick me up at five. I love the trails out at Audubon.

I go back upstairs and get ready. My hair is longer, so I put it up in a rubber band. I decide on shorts because it's a little warmer outside today; maybe some of the guys from school will be out there. I'm really wishing the new guy that Debbie is crushing on is out there too. I get done with the hair and clothes making sure I look good, make my bed and head downstairs. I let Mom know I'm ready and go into the kitchen to grab a banana to eat. I ate a big breakfast, eggs, bacon, sausage, biscuits and gravy, around eight this morning, so I'm not really ready for anything else right now.

"You ready Ria?" my mom asks with a big smile on her face. I nod my head yes. "Sophia get in the car and buckle up," Mom tells my sister. She is already whining to go with me, I just look at my mom with eyes that relay I don't want her with me today. I love my sister, I really do, but she is three years younger, and she wants to do everything with me. I just want to hang with my bestie today.

My mom smiles. "Sophia, not today honey," she says in a voice that you just don't question.

I smile and mouth 'thank you' without a sound.

It takes us about twenty minutes to get to the park, and when we pull up, I see Debbie ahead of us. Looks like Pete is dropping her off.

"Ria, don't leave from the park. I will be back at five to pick you up, okay?" mom says.

"Okay, Mom," I respond and with a smile, I lean over and give her a kiss. I go to open the door, lean back over and give her a big hug. "I love you, Momma. I'll see you here at five."

I have a great mom. She always listens to me, no matter what. I get out of the car and yell at Debbie. She waves and we meet up. Pete is yelling, "Did you hear me Debbie? Don't leave here."

"Yes, I heard you the first time you yelled out at me; *I understand, Dad*," she yells sarcastically. Yep, sounds just like her. They must have been going at it again. Since Pete got on at the local sheriff's office, he has gotten bossier.

We meet up and I give her a hug. "Is Pete, being a jerk again?" I ask.

"Yeah. I am so done with it. Watch my back, watch for strangers, don't talk to anyone we don't know. Same stuff since he became a cop. I am so sick of it. He told Mom we shouldn't be coming out here by ourselves. Mom finally told him to hush. It wouldn't hurt any to let us go walking," Debbie says, partly mocking Pete's voice.

She hands me a bottle of water and we decide to go to the bathroom before we head out. We head in and are talking about what we want to do this summer. We for sure want to go to Holiday World, a local theme park; it isn't too far from us. We're washing our hands when she asks me if I think she's pretty.

"Debbie, I don't understand why you always ask me this. You are so pretty. I love your hair. I'd love for my hair to look like yours, long, red, and a little curly. Why are you asking me this again?" I ask.

"Well, I kinda like that new boy from our math class. You know the one that came during the last month of school. He is soooo cute. Don't ya think?" She giggles.

"Yeah, I know the one. Why don't you call and ask him if he wants to hang out with you?" I tell her.

"I don't want to make a fool of myself. What if he thinks I'm ugly or something?" she moans.

"Won't know until you ask," I mutter. "Look, he would be so lucky to be asked out by you. You are so pretty," I tell her in a teenage dramatic girlish voice.

"You think?" she questions yet again. I nod my head. We leave the bathroom and head out. We talk and walk the trails for the next two hours. I ask her if she wants to come spend the night with me. She says she needs to ask her mom, but she wants to. We had a great afternoon talking and cutting up. Her brothers are all at home and are driving her crazy. I honestly love all of them, and they treat me just like they do Debbie. They can be so funny and bossy, and they like to play board games and watch television with us.

As we're heading out of the last trail, for some reason I have chills going up and down my arms and neck.

"Ria are you okay? You look a little funny." Debbie stops walking.

I nod as I tell her, "I am fine. Just got chilled for a minute," I mumble.

As we start walking, I'm looking down at the ground because this trail is really uneven as you come out of it. Debbie is right behind me; this is an extremely narrow area and only one can go through it at a time. I take the first step out and as I look forward, there is an old dark van sitting there. Looks like no one is in it. That seems strange. I hear Debbie cry out and turn to see

4

what's wrong. I see a shadow as I am hit on the side of my head. I go down on my hands and knees not understanding what's happening. Debbie is sobbing. I can't concentrate as I hear her yell out and then silence. I am shaking my head trying to focus and I'm hit again and lifted up over someone's shoulder. I think I hear two voices, but I can't stay focused long enough to understand anything. I don't even hear the birds anymore. I keep asking what's going on. Last thing I remember is hitting the floor of the van, and Debbie screaming.

∽

LIBBY'S POV

I'm at the park where I dropped off Ria three hours ago. Debbie's mom, Jackie, pulls up next to me. We both get out and start talking while waiting on the girls. We've been talking for some time when I look at my watch. It's now five forty-five.

"Jackie, it's getting really late. The girls are always on time. *Always*," I say in a scared voice.

"I know, Libby. I think I'm going to call Neil and have him come out so we can go look for them," Jackie says.

"I'll call Astor too." I dial the number at home and before he can say a word, I'm crying and talking as fast as I can. He has to tell me to slow down so that he can understand me. "Honey, I've been here for an hour waiting on Ria, she isn't here, and I'm worried."

I hear Jackie telling Neil the same thing. I grab Sophia out of the car as we start walking around the main area asking if anyone has seen them. I had forgotten to grab a picture from my wallet, so I was describing her and Debbie both. We continued to look, but so far no one has seen either one of them. I had one lady tell me she had seen them over two hours ago on the one trail, furthest from the restrooms. She showed me which one, by taking us to it. Both Neil and Astor have shown up. We are by our vehicles, so I grab a picture of Ria and Jackie gets a recent one of Debbie. They tell us to question people as they come off the trails. They go down that last trail that the girls were seen on.

They get back an hour later. They found water bottles on the ground as they were coming off the trail. Neil seems to think they were the girls, so we decide to call the police. Neil has called his boys, although Pete is working, he has dispatch call him as well. The police and family all start showing up at the same time. Jackie and I are both a mess but holding it together. At midnight they call the search off until six in the morning. We all go home. As I remember that Astor's sister hasn't been notified of what's going on up to this point, I have Astor call and let her know we will call tomorrow with any updates as there are none tonight. I fall back onto the couch and watch as the clock slowly ticks away as I stare at the door and window hoping for a miracle that she just got lost and comes home. I sit there all night with Astor, his arms around me as I rock with tears slowly rolling down my face. Every once in a while, I sob. Astor continues to hold me and when I snivel, he does too. We are still on the couch when we get a call at five letting us know that the search is on standby because of the rain. They said it isn't safe. I think, *if it isn't safe for us to search, it isn't for my baby either.*

We're told to stay by the phones, and they would call as soon as they start the search. It's seven and still raining, it hasn't stopped or slowed down any.

At eight thirty-four that morning the doorbell rings. We are both startled, I think we dozed off a little. We jump and race to the door. It's Pete.

"Any news, Pete?" I ask with tears in my eyes, lips trembling. My grip on his arm is strong but shaking uncontrollably from the lack of sleep and nerves. Not knowing anything is slowly draining me both physically and mentally.

"Libby, Astor." He nods. "Let's sit down for a moment."

I look at Astor, sob, and start to collapse to the ground. He grabs me up and leads me to the couch.

"Please just tell me. Do you know where my baby is?" I ask with desperation in my voice.

"About thirty minutes ago, someone found Debbie in a ditch. She's alive but badly beaten. Right now, they're taking her to the hospital. This is what I know—Debbie said that as they were coming off that one trail where the water bottles were found, and someone knocked her from behind. She vaguely remembers Ria hollering out. While she was on the ground, she had seen Ria there too. The next thing she remembers is that both of them were thrown into the back of the van. It was dark in color and that is about all I know. She has no idea where Ria is now. She did say that the guy was talking wildly. Like he was crazy. We have an all-points bulletin out. The FBI has been called in because it's so close to the state line.

There's a good possibility that it's been crossed," he tells us with a wobbly voice. "The FBI is going to be here very soon to set up a line so if anyone calls, they can trace it."

"I need to see Debbie," I sob, falling into Astor's arms. "I need to talk to her," I say with a wild cry.

The doorbell rings—it's the FBI.

CHAPTER ONE

"Dammit, Sassy, let me in the door before I trip. Just a minute and I'll pick you up. Jeez, you would think you haven't seen me in a month." It has been seven hours but still. Picking her up I take her toward the back door to let her outside to go potty. I head back in to the front door, stop and make sure that I re-locked it, and pick up the shit I dropped on the floor while being attacked by my four-and-a-half-pound Yorkie with a black and silver body and white face. I take the groceries that I stopped and bought, and I start putting them away. I really wasn't hungry, so, I grab a glass of sweet tea and let Sassy, who was scratching on the door, back in.

The phone starts ringing.

"Hello," I answer.

"Hi, honey. How was your day at work?" my mom asks.

"It was good, Mom. Long but I got through all my clients on time. I saw your friend Meri today. She just wanted her hair washed and set. She also made an appointment for some func-tion she said you and she are attending in two weeks. So, it looks like I get to see your friend two weeks in a row. I feel so privileged, Mom. I guess they're having some sort of a fundraiser for cancer. A bunch of them smut-writing authors that the both of you like are having a signing and donating the money."

"I can't understand why you don't read these books with me and your sister. It's called 'Authors and Dancers Against Cancer.' Last year, she said they raised well over three thousand dollars."

"Have fun, Mom," I say with a snicker. We talked for a little while longer and hung up. My mom, Libby, calls my sister Sophia and me at least every other day to check up on us. Astor Comis is my daddy and his family hails from Greece. Although he's an American, he has the Greek personality. The women in my family are both blondes. Daddy's hair is a shade or two darker brown than mine, it's also shorter than mine; mine goes to the middle of my back. I'm about five feet four and weigh one hundred and thirty-five pounds.

I own my own business and have four other stylists that rent space at my salon, *Unique Styles*. I have owned my own business for the last two years. It has grown by leaps and bounds. We set our own hours, although we make sure that someone is always working from nine to five daily and Saturday from nine to noon. I have a large client base and can sometimes see up to twenty people in one day.

Laura, Mary, Becky and Alexis don't have as many clients, but they keep just as busy. These ladies are a part of my family. They are all married but Laura is getting a divorce from a man that just isn't in love with her anymore. According to her, anyway. That left me the odd person out in the group.

I have been in one relationship and he was verbally abusive. It lasted all of about six months and I kicked his ass to the curb. Last date I went on, I left in the middle of the date. He was a hand-grabbing piece of shit. We hadn't even sat down for dinner and he was expecting some pussy, his words not mine, and that wasn't happening.

As I sit here watching the news on a Friday night with nothing to do, I holler at my baby girl. "Come here, Sassy. Let's watch some tv together." She looks at me, ignoring me as she trots down the hallway. Shaking my head, I get up to gather my weekly laundry and get it done. I clean my little two-bedroom cottage home for the week and put my laundry away. I decide now it's not too early to take my shower and head to bed for the night. Talking to myself, *I need to find myself a beefed-up man cake. I want to find a tattooed, muscled beefcake that rides a Harley. Wouldn't that just shock the hell out of everyone.* As I am drifting away to sleep, I think, *In my dreams!*

If I only knew then…

I wake up with the sun shining through the cracks of my mini blinds. Sassy is dancing all around me on the bed getting her morning hugs in. I get up to go to the bathroom and finish washing my hands. Sassy is trying to crawl up my legs. I stoop and pick her up on my way to let her out for her morning business. I go make myself a cup of hot coffee. I take my first sip as my childhood friend Debbie calls wanting to know if I would go with her after work, so she can get a tattoo. I agree and set up a time to meet around four o'clock that afternoon at my house. I let Sassy in and feed her as I go get ready for my half-day at the salon.

I make it to work just in time to get things ready before my first client walks through the door.

"Hey, Laura, how was your night?"

"Good, I guess. Dick came in and left with his buddies. Said they were going to play pool. Whatever. I wish he would move out already and let me get on with my life. He can't have it both ways."

"He was named Dick for a reason. You should have realized that at the time, that he would be one too. Did he come back home?" I ask.

"About seven this morning, and I probably shouldn't have married him, but it's not because of his small penis either," she says smiling.

"It's time for him to hit the road," I tell her as I laugh out loud.

"I'm going to tell him when I get back home that he has one month. I am so done with this shit," Laura says.

"I have to get shit set up for my first client. Are you busy today?" I ask.

"I have only six coming in today with my last one coming in at eleven, so I'll clean up before I leave for the day," states Laura.

"I have three until ten o'clock. I can do some walk-ins if you need me too. Then, I'm going to catch up on paperwork until about noon. I'll be out of here until Tuesday," I say.

As I head toward the back, Laura sits her first client down for her wash and set. I go and get things together and have it all ready for when Gwen walks in the door. She is a regular client and always comes in for a color and cut every six weeks. We talk as I start. She is one of my favorites. I do what I like with her hair. She likes to switch things up. I usually let her know ahead of time of what I'm planning.

As the morning wears on, I see people walking up and down the sidewalk of our community of Henderson, Kentucky. It's about the size of forty-six thousand people in the county. Not large but not small either. The streets are lined with wooden planters that are filled each year with different flowers by the town committee.

I can see the shop owners sweeping up outside their doors

before the Saturday morning shoppers descend. Laura turns on the radio and we hear the morning announcer talking about the 'Authors and Dancers Against Cancer' event coming up in two weeks. He says that they are having raffle baskets and about eighty authors on hand for Saturday's event. All types of dancers will have a recital on the Friday night before the signing.

I think to myself that I may go to the recital. It sounds like a great cause, even if I did kind of laugh at Mom last night on the phone. I am a smut-reading, closet junkie. If my mom only knew.

I finish up my morning clients and head to the back to get the weekly supply paperwork done so I can re-order for the next week. I grab my clipboard and start humming as familiar tunes come on the radio.

Next thing I know, I hear Laura letting me know she's all done and locking up for the day.

I get my things put together then head back and I review the order supply one more time and then hit submit. They will be delivered early Tuesday morning. The shop is always closed on Sundays and open by appointment only on Mondays.

As I walk out the door, I stop and take in the beautiful day. Warm sunny blue skies without a cloud in sight. I decide to pick up a few plants on my way home for the planters on my front porch. I hop into my Honda and down the road I go. I stop by the local nursery and pick up twelve plants.

It's three o'clock and I just got done planting my flowers on the porch. I grab a quick ham and cheese sandwich and love on Sassy a little. I jump in the shower and get cleaned up for my outing with Debbie to the tattoo parlor. I have always wanted a lot of tattoos and know what I want. I've had my drawings for the last six years. I keep them in my purse so if I ever get the guts, I'm ready. That's not happened yet. I grab some jeans and pull out one of my favorite tees. It's one with some prickly cactuses on the front saying, "I am ready for some hugs." I am pulling on my shoes as Debbie knocks on the door.

"Come in, Debbie."

"Hey Katarina," she says as she smirks.

I look at her with a raised eyebrow. "You know one of these days you're going to call me that and I'm going to kick your ass."

"That's your name," she says laughing.

"Like I said, Deborah," drawing her name out slow, "one of these days."

We both laugh as I go to let Sassy in. Sassy eyes Debbie and she is all over her. Running around in circles and yapping like a magpie. I finally get her settled down and out the door we go as I shut and lock it.

"Are you driving, or am I?" I ask her.

"I am," she says.

"Okay, let's go," I tell her.

I notice as we walk out to her Jeep that she already as her top and doors off. We climb in and head down the road going toward one of the newest tattoo parlors in town. It's been there longer than my shop but it's the newest one around in the surrounding counties. I have been past their shop just a few times. Scoping it out, hoping one of these days that I have the guts to stop, finally. As we're going down the street, we talk about how our week has gone. Debbie stands about five foot nine and is stick straight with a few slight curves in just the right places. She has the most gorgeous green eyes I have ever seen with long red hair that she keeps piled on top of her head all the time. She weighs maybe one-forty sopping wet. She has a great sense of humor and she needs it coming from a family of all brothers, four to be exact. She is the youngest at twenty-five, like me. I love her parents like they're my own as she does mine. Her brothers are my brothers, Sophia my sister is hers too.

"So, what kind of tattoo are you getting this time?" I ask her.

"Well, I'll show you when we get there."

"Okkkkay," I respond.

As we get close to our destination, I notice she keeps glancing at me. I look at her and say, *"What?"*

"Nothing," she responds.

She glances forward as she's pulling into the parking slot right in front of the building. The parlor has a large sign out front that says in bold gold and black lettering *Ink-Fusions*.

The sign is hanging on an L-shaped overhang over the doorway. The window is large with big black scripted lettering 'Permanent Facial Makeup, Tattoos and Piercings. Owner, Jax Rawlings, Hours Tuesday through Saturday, Eleven A.M. to Seven P.M. All other hours are by appointment only.'

The building is a medium-red colored brick, with a walkway between two buildings that runs to the back alley. As I take it all in, Debbie looks at me and says, "Did you bring your purse?"

"Well of course I brought it. I always carry my purse with me. You know that." I look at her like she's lost her mind.

"Good," she says. "Let me see your drawings."

"Why would I let you see my drawings? You've already seen them a million times," I tell her.

"Ummmm, well, cause the appointment is yours, not mine," she states, looking at me with a grin on her face.

"What in the ever-loving hell are you talking about Debbie? You better hope and pray you're joking."

"No, I am not. You have wanted one for the last six years and I paid for you to get your first one today. You have about five minutes before your appointment and I'm here to make sure you go through with it," she says with a serious look on her face.

"I am going to string you up and drag you down the road behind your own Jeep," I say with a mean glint in my eyes.

She has absolutely lost her ever-loving mind. There is no way I'm getting a tattoo today.

She looks at me with a determined look on her face and tells me, "Oh yes you are, it's no different from when you made an appointment for me to have my hoochie koochie clitty pierced last year."

I knew that was going to come back and bite me in the ass one day. *Well fuck me running,* I think.

"Let's go, Deborah Sue," I tell her with a sly grin on my face.

CHAPTER TWO

We are almost to the door when this lady with long black hair pulled back in a French braid comes down the sidewalk from two doors down carrying what looks to be four cups of coffee. The one is in a clear plastic glass and it looks like a frappe with whipped cream.

I should have made Debbie stop so I could pick up a frappe with whipped crème too. I may have her go get me one if I am doing this today. As we hold open the door, she looks at me and smiles and says, "Thank you." Her hair is full and shiny. I wish mine looked like that. I walk to the counter, as the same lady sets the coffee down and I am asked if I have an appointment. I look at her and tell her, "I suppose, that's what I've been led to believe, anyway."

She looks at me with her eyebrows raised and Debbie says, "She does. Name is Ria Comis, she has an appointment for four-thirty." She looks at me, then Debbie. I could hear the wheels in her head turning.

"My name is Samantha," she says. "I have some forms I need

you to fill out, Ria. Did you bring in your design like you said you would when you made your appointment?" she asks me.

"I didn't make the appointment, but yes I do have some designs," I state.

"Designs? You have more than one?" she asks.

"I do. I'm not sure which one I would like first," I tell her.

"That's okay, go ahead and fill out your paperwork and I'll let Jax know you're here, Ria," she states.

She picks up the drinks she brought in and heads toward the back. I can hear music as well as several machines going. People normally just call them tattoo guns. Small talk can be heard in the background as I fill out my form. Debbie has already gone and copped a squat in one of the chairs with a big grin on her face. I just look at her, give her that evil smile and she turns her head. She knows that evil look of mine and payback is a bitch. I turn around and see Samantha coming back up front. She looks in the seating area and tells some young girl that she can come back. Samantha asks her if she brought the earrings that she wanted put in with her or did she need to look at what was available. The girl told her she had some.

Samantha looks at me and tells me that Jax is just about done and will be with me in just a minute. She heads back to the rear with the young girl and I hear them talking in low voices. As I glance around, I notice a bunch of photos on the wall with lots of people and tattoos. I spot a photo of a man in one, and I swear I can feel my panties get wet.

As I walk closer to the photo, I swear my heart picks up and my mouth starts to water. OMG... My dream man... My beefcake honey pie dream man. Look at them muscles, all them tattoos, nice thick beard—thick enough to grab onto as I ride his face. He has a piercing in his nose too.

I wonder if he has one down south too. What I wouldn't give to find out. As I am standing here in this daze, I finally hear this voice behind me asking if I'm okay.

As I am staring at the photo I say, "Why wouldn't I be alright? This is the best I've felt in a long time. Why do you ask?"

"Well, Ria, you were moaning like you were in pain and you have what looks like drool coming down the side of your face."

"You don't have epilepsy, do you?" he asks.

"No," I say, still staring at the picture.

As I slowly turn from the photo, I look up and there he stands.

"My dream man," I'm thinking. He looks at me with a faint smirk on his face.

"Dream man? Tell me more," he says. I stand there and my jaw drops down.

"Please tell me I didn't say that out loud," I state.

"Ummmm, you did," he says, with this indescribable look on his face.

I take my hand and slap the palm of it against my face.

"I am so embarrassed," I tell him.

"Don't be," he says with a smile on his face.

His voice just made me cream my panties more. All I can do is stare at him. After a minute of just staring at his mesmerizing sparkling brown eyes, he asks me if I'm ready.

"Ready, for what?" I ask.

He smiles at me and says come on let's go. I'm thinking, I will go wherever you want. I turn and look at Debbie and she has a big ass grin on her face. I smile back, in a dazed state. I should have come here a long time ago.

I sit in his chair and he asks if I have any idea of what I want. I pull out my sketches and give them to him. He sees the picture of some tribal designs I like. Pictures of a big cross. The last is a picture of a miniature dragon that I have wanted since the beginning. I had drawn it while I was in college. I want it placed on my side from rear to front rib. It does need some female aspects put with it to make it more feminine.

He stares at the dragon, then looks at me.

"I like this," he says. "Do you know where you want this?"

"I want it placed on my side from my rear hip up through my side ending on my ribs in the front. I want something with it to make it more feminine though. I just never figured out what would make it that way," I say as I look him in the eyes.

"Trust me?" he says, and I nod yes. "Let me go work on it for a few minutes and I'll come back." I nod my head. Still too dazed to say much of anything else, I look around his workspace and see more designs hanging on the walls with tacks. I also see a lot of bottles with color, spray bottles and rolls of paper towels. Everything looks so clean, white, and sterile. A Sharps container sits in the corner on the cabinet. A black chair is large enough to sit a four-hundred-pound person and it lays down as well as reclines. Pictures are lined along the wall, one that looks like his parents, I see a strong family resemblance. He's in it, so it must be his sister and brother too.

As I sit here, I can hear others working and wonder how many are here. I can't believe Debbie did this. She must have planned this a while back.

Jax comes back in and shows me the picture. The drawing I did is the same, but he's added a few vines with flowers and gems intermixed in the design. I gasp.

"This is beautiful," I state. *This is exactly what I want.*

"So, do you want this one?" he asks.

"Do bears shit in the woods?" I state. My face turns a little red. I can't help it. This shit just comes out of my mouth so naturally, I forget sometimes to curb my smartass remarks.

His laugh makes a booming sound. I see the twinkle in his eyes as well as the smile on his face and I just fall that much faster. My daddy always told me I would fall fast and hard.

Jax takes the transfer paper and has me lie on my side. He gets his supplies for my tattoo all set up, cleans my skin and then applies the transfer to my skin. I get up to make sure it's where I want it and if I like it. I love it and I'm so excited.

I lie there as he begins, and he tells me what he's doing, as well as explains kind of what I am going to feel. I feel the pinch of the needle as it runs across my skin. At first it hurts like little stings from a bee and then I really don't feel much of anything. I lay there and daydream, coming out of it when he asks me if I'm okay. He told me it would take two to three sessions to get it finished. I'm there about forty minutes when I drift off to sleep. An hour and a half later, he shakes me awake.

"Hey, beautiful, it's time to wake up," he says, with a smile on his face. He tells me that there aren't many people that will zone out the way I did through this process and fall asleep. I look at him and smile. He tells me to look in the mirror before he wraps me up. It looks really good. He gets me cleaned up with anti-bacterial soap, applies ointment on it, and then wraps it in clear handi-wrap type material. He gives me the instructions on how to take care of it. He takes my hand squeezing it and walks me to the front.

Samantha is up there talking to Debbie, and I hear Debbie tell her that she wants another piercing. Where? I have no idea. She is already riddled with them. Samantha tells her anytime, just call.

He tells Samantha to schedule a new appointment for me, while his eyes never leave mine. I look at Jax and smile. He leans down and whispers in my ear that he'll talk to me later, turns and heads to the back. I'm at a loss of words right about now. I don't know what to say or think. I watch him go and mutter, *"Kauto"*.

"There she goes talking in Greek," Debbie says with a big grin. "What did you just say?"

I reply, "Hot."

I turn back around, and Samantha and Debbie are grinning like loons.

"What?" I ask with a smile.

Samantha shakes her head and states, "Nothing. Just nothing. He looks like he's into you is all, and it's good to see." I turn and glare at Debbie and ask her the same thing. She holds both hands up and says, "Not a thing."

I let her know I need another appointment for Friday evening or sometime Saturday.

I make my appointment, and Debbie and I head out the door. Debbie looks at me and asks me if I'm okay.

"Well that depends on what you mean by okay. My side is a little sore, I've made a mess in my panties and I didn't even get a kiss. Sure, he had his hands all over my body, but not where I wanted. My God, Debbie, he is *hot*, I mean steamy *hot*… This has been the best day," I tell her as I moan out loud.

"Really?" she asks me with wonder in her voice.

"Yes, really," I reply with a small grin.

Debbie laughs, and we get in her Jeep. I keep staring at the building as we back out. She asks me if I want to grab a bite to eat, so we head to a local restaurant for dinner.

Later in the evening, I recall my conversation with Debbie. She had been there before for piercings and had seen Jax. She knew what my dream man looked like from my description and decided to put things in action. I guess we'll wait and see what happens, because I am ready to go back.

I shower and get ready for bed. I mess with my baby, Sassy. I love that dog. She is so full of mischief just like her momma. I can't wait to see Jax next Saturday. He got a lot accomplished today. Maybe only one more session and it should be done, but I'm hoping for two. If not, I guess I'll be getting a lot of tattoos done.

The week is long, but it's finally Friday and I have the weekend off. I take every other one off so that we all get time off with our families. Alexis does the ordering when I'm not there. She always sends me an email with the order for my approval, but it's not needed. She knows what she's doing and what we need. I'm home and change out of my work clothes. I have played with Sassy for a while and have been thinking of Jax. I even looked him up on the internet. He is a well-known artist that works on women who have had breast cancer as well as other clients for different types of cancer and conditions. I never would have guessed. He's also recommended by some of the doctors in the tri-state area. Am I a stalker? I say no, I'm just someone that's interested in the man who's working on my body and needs to be well-informed. I'm laughing at myself now, as I think this. He never called like I thought he might, but something just tells me, this sense, deep in my gut feeling that he's interested.

Debbie calls and asks if I'm going tomorrow. Duh, of course I am. She lets me know she has to work through the day. She tells me she'll stop by tomorrow night about nine. I tell her okay.

I've slept like the dead with no dreams to whet my appetite, although I am refreshed and ready to get this show on the road. I have my weekly chores to do as well as my monthly bills that need to be paid.

I drink my morning cup of coffee, then get another as I get ready for the day. I finally put on a pair of jean shorts with a flimsy tee. It's lilac in color with some light-colored outlines of flowers on it. I start my chores and start my laundry for the week as I sit down to pay the bills.

It's about twelve and I just can't wait any longer. My thoughts and male candy cravings are at an all-time high, I am ready to go. I finish up my last-minute things and grab my purse on my way out the door. I take my outgoing mail down to the mailbox. I get back in my car, turn on my music, open the sunroof, and away I go. It takes me about thirty minutes because of an accident in town.

I pull in and notice a couple of people go in, as one comes out. I hop out and head inside to see Jax at the counter. He looks up as I enter, and he smiles just for me. He tells Samantha he has thirty minutes before his next appointment, and he'll be back. He comes around the corner and grabs my hand as he's going out the door.

"Where are we going?" I ask.

"We're going to go grab a bite to eat before my next appointment," he replies.

"I am your appointment." I smirk.

"I know, but I'm hungry, so let's go, beautiful," he states.

We head to a place called *Tacoholics*, a block over and around the corner. It's a big orange building with a bunch of tables. We order and talk about everyday things.

We have been here about thirty minutes when I just ask him. I can't seem to help myself.

"Tell me about yourself," I ask him.

He replies with, "Samantha told me your friend made the appointment for you. We need to finish your tattoo though, because I don't normally mix business with pleasure. I want to get to know you too... since I am your dream man.

"I want to get to know you too, but in order to do that, you have to talk to me. I can't read your mind," I state.

He asks me if I'm done with lunch. I am, so I tell him yes, I'm ready. It's time to finish up my tattoo. This is the strangest way I have ever met anyone. It's like a story, a fake one at that, just like in my smut books I keep hidden from everyone. I shake my head. He grabs my hand, and out the door we go after he pays for the meal.

As we leave and go back, I'm thinking, I hope this isn't another Hedrick Bishop. That man if you want to call him that was off his rocker. He was the nicest guy until about four months into the relationship. He became verbally abusive that eventually turned physical. Trent, Debbie's brother who is like my brother too, had stopped by one day while he was home visiting his parents. Hedrick was there screaming and hollering. That was the day he raised his fist and hit me in the chest. Talk about Rambo going off on his ass. I thought Trent was going to kill him. Trent rides with a one-percenter club a couple of hours southeast of Henderson. I haven't seen Hedrick since. I will have to ask Debbie when Trent is coming back. We need to go down and see him at the clubhouse soon. We go down about every two months, to family gatherings. I miss the guys at the clubhouse, they're like a second family to me. That's about the only time we're allowed there.

Jax and I get back to the shop and head to the back. Samantha hollers, "Hello," and smiles. Some guy looks up from his work, looks at us, and nods his chin. Jax does the same. A few more steps and a man comes out of the back room.

"Well, who do we have here.?" he says. It kind of reminded me of 'who do we have here, my pretty.'

"I'm Ria, and you are?" I state.

Jax keeps tugging me along as he says, "He is no one."

"I'm Jax's younger brother Toby," he says with a grin. "Are you the one he keeps talking about? The Dragon lady? He hasn't acted this way in a long time, at least not since bitch face anyway," he mutters under his breath.

"Samantha wasn't lying when she said you were gorgeous. How old are you and where do you live? Are you nice? Cause if not, you need to kick it," he says seriously.

Jax finally stops. Since he's dragging me, and not letting me walk down the hallway, I plow into him. "Will you shut the fuck up? Not another word. Not one or I will fire your ass," Jax spits out with gritted teeth as he pushes Toby backwards.

Toby looks at Jax and tells him, "I'm just looking out for you."

Jax is red in the face, and he looks mad as hell.

Jax does the introductions. He introduces me as his girlfriend. *We haven't even been on a date, and now I'm his girlfriend?* My mouth falls open on this piece of information.

I look from one to the other. I tell Jax, "It's okay."

He stands there and says, "No it's not." I don't understand

26

what's going on here. Toby has this serious look on his face and Jax is just staring him down.

"If you so much as think of calling Mom, not only will you not have a job, I will kick your ass from here to Timbuktu. You understand me?" Jax spits out.

"I won't say a word," Toby replies.

All this time, I'm thinking girlfriend, threatening his brother and he isn't to tell his mom. I don't understand this part. This is just mind boggling.

Jax continues walking, tugging on my arm, as I follow him into his room. I look back at Toby with a smile and wave.

I sit in his chair and I notice he already has everything set up for my tattoo. "Lie on your side again. Are you ready?"

I nod my head. I ask him, "What was all of that about?"

"I will tell you all about it later."

I ask him again, "Are you seeing anyone?"

He assured me he wasn't. We're there for about three hours when he turns off his iron.

"I'm done, it looks magnificent," he states. I get up and turn to look in the mirror. I am in awe. It's more than I thought it ever could be. I love it. Reds, black, purples, blues, yellows, and greens are mixed in the tattoo.

I turn back around and reach up to give him a hug. He grabs me, picks me up and kisses me like I never have been before. His tongue is velvet soft; his lips are so smooth. I feel a little puff of his breath as he continues to learn all the crevices of my mouth. His taste, just a slight hint of mint. I feel his beard across my face as he devours my mouth and lips. I need air, I can't think. I feel faint. He lifts his head, looks at me with glistening lips and tells me we're going out tonight. He doesn't ask, he tells me in a demanding voice. Secretly that's what I've been wanting—a demanding male. I don't want someone that's weak. I need a man to be a man and not some weakling that belittles and hits me. He must own me. I continue to look at him with wide eyes and a wet mouth. He sets me down and starts to clean up the tattoo and adds the salve so he can wrap it up. He tells me to give him a few, as he cleans up his area. I take the bottle of Lysol from his hand and start cleaning the chairs and the other counters. He places the rest of his things up and I go wipe and spray down those counters too. He bundles his trash and says he'll be right back.

Five minutes later we are ready to leave. "Do you have any more clients?" I ask quizzically.

"It's my day off." He looks at me to see my expression.

Wow is all I can think; he finished my tat on his day off. I have a beaming smile on my face.

"Give me a minute to come around to the front, and I will follow you home." I nod agreeing.

As I'm waiting, I talk to Samantha. Toby comes out to say goodbye and also to apologize. I tell him not to worry about it, I think it's cool he looks out for his family. I hear rumbles in the distance but they are getting closer. We all turn around and watch as three motorcycles pull up. The men get off and come inside. Big, muscled men, wearing cuts. I look to see if I know them. I don't recognize the emblem on the cuts. I will have to ask Trent if he knows of any clubs in the area. I see Jax pull up in a car. It's a blue Dodge Charger. He stops, looks inside the shop, parks and heads in, what seems really fast.

"Can I help you out fellas?" he asks the man wearing the VP patch.

The guy with the VP patch holds out his hand. "Name is Dog," he replies. "Was told that I needed to look up Jax when I got here."

"That's me," Jax replies.

"I was told you're one of the best artists around and I need some work done," Dog says. He pulls out a paper with a drawing on it.

Jax looks at it and says, "I can do that but not today. It's my day off and I have plans. I can work on it if you want to leave it with me," he tells Dog.

Dog tells him he can make it worth his while if he could do it today. Jax says no again. Finally, Jax tells the guy that his plans can't be undone. He tells Dog to come in next week on Wednesday and he'll get him in first thing. Dog finally agrees and leaves after Samantha puts him on the books.

As we watch them leave, Samantha states that they have a one-percent patch on. I look at her wondering how she knows that. To my knowledge, there are no clubs nearby. Jax tells the three bikers to be careful, and to leave together.

We head out and he follows me home. It doesn't take near as long as it did coming into town. I live on the outskirts of town, on the north side, out off Route 60, on a side street, past Walmart. It would normally only take about ten minutes if I come in off the parkway. It's soon to be Interstate 69, and with all the road construction it takes much longer to get where you want to go in town.

I park my car, get out, and make sure my car doors are locked. Jax is out of his car and right behind me. I stop to unlock the door first. As we head in the house, I scoop up Sassy before she runs out the door.

"What the hell is that?" he asks.

"This is my baby, Sassy. She thinks that everyone should dote on her and that she's the queen of the house," I tell him with a laugh.

Sassy jumps from my arms to his and starts licking his face. He follows me as I go toward the back door. I open it, take Sassy from his arms, and put her outside.

CHAPTER THREE

He shuts my door, and turns and swoops in, lips on lips, mouth on mouth. I love the feel of his juicy lips on mine.

"You taste like peaches, Ria. I can't get enough. Your skin is so soft," he tells me while running his hands up and down my arms and shoulders. He gently rubs them under the sleeve of my shirt.

He pauses, like he is in a transfixed state. I stand, my arms wrapped around his broad-muscled shoulders. I wait. I have no idea what he's thinking. I watch as emotions run across his face.

"I have thought of nothing else but you all week," he tells me in a low voice. "I think of you all the time unless I mess up and think of that bitch, Vivian. I'm so sorry for bringing this up with you in my arms. I need to tell you about her and what she has done to me. She warped my mind and I told myself I would never give a woman that kind of power over me ever again. She had my child aborted, but then told me she had a miscarriage. It was a great big mind fuck. At the time I didn't want kids, but she convinced me that she wanted to keep it. After I got all excited about my little girl, she does the unimaginable and gets rid of her. She went to another state thinking I wouldn't find out. She was far enough along that they knew the sex of my child. Why do that if she didn't want her to begin with? I pray one day she rots in Hell for what she did. She started messing around two weeks afterwards. Slept with my so-called best friend, John. I always said he would pay for it and he did. He called apologizing a year ago, after she did the same thing to him. The only difference was, he was married to her at the time. She's never going to change, and I stay clear of places I know she frequents. John thought he could just come back to the way it was before he fucked her and be my friend again. No, never. I have no use for him. I trusted him and he broke that trust." He takes a breath and continues, "Fuck, I need to quit thinking of all this shit."

"Are you okay? I know bringing up old memories can fuck with your head." We head into the living room and sit on the couch. We face each other with our knees touching.

"I'm okay," he says.

"I need to talk to you about some things before these feelings between us goes any further. I think you know what I am talking about. I don't want to get into this and then find out you have someone on the sidelines," he tells me.

"I don't have anyone on the sidelines and I'm listening Jax," I tell him.

"As I mentioned, Vivian started messing around with John, my best friend at the time. I kicked them both to the curb. A year ago, I get this call from John, he's crying telling me she did the same thing to him. He kept telling me he was so sorry. I told him he was on his own, although I did tell him I was sorry about the baby."

I sit there waiting for him to continue. He just stares ahead, then tilts his head forward and stares at me for a long time.

"If we do this, I will not and cannot abide any sort of cheating. All bets are off. So, if you have anyone on the sidelines tell me now… *I refuse to share.*" He tells me with more determination not only in his body language but his voice as well. I have never heard this from anyone before.

"I am all in Jax, I want to see where this goes, I also have my own issues but am nowhere ready to talk about them with you yet." I whisper as I lean in to kiss him. Just about that time I hear Sassy at the back door just going nuts. She isn't stopping, and it sounds like she's hurt. I go running to the back door and there she is with her tongue hanging out. I open the door and she trots in like she doesn't have a care in the world. The old saying 'cock-blocker' is now 'kiss blocker.'

Jax starts laughing at her antics. He asks, "What do you want to do?"

"Debbie is coming over at nine, I didn't know we were going out. She had asked, and I told her to come on over," I tell him with regret.

"Let's go out for dinner and a small car ride. I will get you back in plenty of time for you to meet up with Debbie," he states. "Tomorrow is mine, I want to spend some time with you, beautiful."

I grin and tell him, "Okay." I clean up a little, and out the door we go. We end up at the *Feed Mill*, the local hotspot in the next county over. They have some of the best food around, and people come from all over to eat there. I order a steak and he orders gator. We share our entrees with each other.

We talk the entire time about our families. I know he has one sister, Cassie, and she lost her high school sweetheart husband in a mining accident. They married when Cassie was eighteen. They have two kids, a girl named Lacy who is eight and a boy named Jake who is seven. Cassie is only twenty-seven and has been a widow since she was twenty-three. Jax told me he spends a lot of time with her and the kids.

We ended up driving for a little over an hour before heading back. We get back and he walks me to the door. He is tugging me to him as we reach the top step. His kisses are some of the best I have ever had. Those lips are pure magic. Rubbing his hands up and down my back, he grips my ass and pulls me forward even more. He's not only moving his mouth but his lower half, and if what I am feeling is truly his, he is more than well blessed. 'This cock of his is so huge!'

Laughing he says, "Yes, I've had no complaints in the dick department. I am well blessed." My face is turning bright red, I choke trying to talk. He takes his hand and taps my back. I really need to stop thinking this stuff, cause apparently, I'm telling him whatever I'm thinking too. He asks if I'm okay, as I nod my head yes.

Two narrow lights sweep across my driveway and as I turn, I see it's Debbie. She must have gotten off a little early. She gets out looking at us. I smile and say hello to her. I look up at Jax. He kisses me again and says he's going to do a walk-through of the house. I hand him my house keys and he unlocks the door, going inside. I wait for Debbie as he unlocks the door and heads in. I look at Debbie and grin real big. The biggest cheesiest grin in the world. She looks at me, grins, and says in a whisper like voice, "I want the deets, girl."

Jax comes back, says he put the Queen in the backyard, and he had already cleared the house.

"Hey, Debbie. How did work go?" he asks her.

With a smile she says, "Good".

She tells me she's going inside. I tell her I'll be with her shortly. I turn and look at Jax, my heart beating in my ears.

"I had a great time tonight. Thank you for dinner too," I tell him.

"I did too. I'll see you in the morning. We will do something. Not sure what yet, I just know I want to spend it with you," he tells me with a sparkle in his brown eyes.

He leans in, tilts my head back with his hand on my chin, and kisses me like there is no tomorrow. He proceeds to kiss my neck, sucking gently on it as he rubs his mouth and tongue up and down my neck. He nibbles on my ear, and softly blows in it. I am so wet. That is the thing that turns me on the most. My ears are an erogenous zone for me. He takes his mouth and it's back on mine. God, he tastes so good. He wraps his arms around me again, I feel him from top to bottom. *Everything*, top to bottom. I moan and he leads me backwards to the side of the house.

His hand finds its way under my shirt. His hands are a dangerous weapon, they feel a little rough as he slides them up and just below my breast on the opposite side of my tattoo. He is so careful to not touch or irritate it as his finger slides up and under my bra as he lifts it. He bends down, nudging my shirt up. His lips start moving on the underside of my tit. He keeps moving upwards, licking and sucking like he has done it a million times to me. His mouth captures the tip, sucking and nipping it. It beads up and my breath has stalled. I feel more than I ever have. He pushes the other side up and repeats, sucking and nipping it too. Both nipples are beaded, and I'm squirming all over his leg. I whine, moan, and beg for more. He stops what he's doing and glances over towards the doorway. I'm grabbing at his head, but he keeps looking away. I glance over and it's, you guessed it, Debbie. She's supposed to be my friend and she's cockblocking me. First my dog, now my friend. This shit has got to stop.

"You bitch," I say.

"You hag," she replies with laughter in her voice.

"What the hell?" I pause. "Why would you interrupt?" I ask her.

"Because Pete called and wanted to know who you were dry humping on the front porch," she replies with a grin. "Pete said he'll have to come over if he gets another complaint from your neighbor." She giggles.

"Who the fuck is Pete?" snarls Jax.

"Pete is Debbie's brother, who in turn is kind of like my big brother," I tell him.

"Why would Pete say he would come over if he got another call from the neighbor?" he asks.

"Because Pete is one of the local deputies in town," I state.

By this time, I am ready to harm someone. I mean hell, I know I'm outside, but *it's my porch*. They can look the other direction. Nosey old lady, she's just jealous. I know she is. I am not making her anymore cookies. I see Mrs. Franks outside her door and yell at her that I am not making her anymore cookies.

She yells back that I will. "I hope you got an eye full Mrs. Franks," I yell at her again.

She starts cackling like an old hen. "I sure did, and it looked hot. Will you take me for a wild ride, young man?" she asks before she turns and goes back inside.

My head lands on Jax's chest as we laugh at this fiasco of a make-out session. Jax starts rubbing my back, and he reaches under my shirt and fixes my bra. He kisses my forehead at the hairline. I lift my face and he kisses my lips one more time. He tells me he will see me tomorrow, and to get enough sleep. He is going to make it a day I will never forget. He walks me to the door, and I turn around telling him goodnight.

I watch him get in his car. As he starts it, I get a chin nod and he heads out. I head inside, and Debbie is on the couch with Sassy, drinking coffee and eating a sandwich. She is trying to look innocent. I look around and it looks like she made me one of each too. Well, it's going to be a long night.

She's like a dog with a bone. Ruff... Ruff. Won't stop until she gets every little last boney detail. I wouldn't trade her for the world, although tonight I want to smack her. Paybacks. Just waiting and thinking, she will get hers.

CHAPTER FOUR

D ebbie starts to shoot out questions faster than a speeding bullet. She doesn't even take a breath as she bounces on the couch. The pillows that were once in the corners are now on the floor. She picks one up, puts it in her lap, and leans forward.

She finally stops, looks at me and squeals like a pig. She acted like she did in the sixth grade when little George kissed me on the lips closed mouth. She acted like it was her he was kissing. She is deprived of male lips I believe. That's it, she needs some lips! Nice fat juicy lips so I can kissblock her ass for once... Ha!

"So, what do you want me to answer first, lizard lips?" I ask with a grin.

"Was it as good as it looked, fuck face?" she replies.

"Better, bitch," I say. "I have never felt this way, Debbie."

"So, are you two going out again? His touch doesn't seem to bother you. I noticed from the beginning. It's like a normal-person relationship," she says with a serious tone.

"I'm his girlfriend according to what he told his brother today, and I feel so safe with him. He touches me and I don't worry with him." I tell her.

Her mouth falls open, her eyes get big and round and she fist bumps the air. See, she likes to live through me. I don't understand it because she is drop dead gorgeous. I know she says she's a stick, but she does have slight curves. Medium height, the prettiest red hair you could imagine, and her tits stand straight out even if she's only a B cup. She has the best personality. She's funny and so kindhearted. She brushes men off; I know some have been interested in her. I have had guys ask me to help them out with setting them up. She won't have it. I don't know what her deal is. She is my very best friend, and I have no idea.

We continue to talk, and I tell her some of what we did. Where we went to eat, what we had. She is so happy for me, especially after Hedrick. I stop and think that I never said anything to Jax about him. I don't want him to think I'm weak. She stays until about one in the morning and then I get ready for bed. I am so tired tonight.

The sun is shining bright into the window through the cracks of the white blinds I have over my windows, but under the turquoise drapes. Sassy is lying across my neck and part of my face. "What the hell is that smell? Smells like busted ass. Are you passing gas, Sassy? Jesus Almighty, stop already." I wonder what she got into. She normally doesn't smell like that unless she gets table food. "Of course," I mutter. Using un-lady like language, I say, "Debbie I am kicking your ass for giving her scraps." I continue to snipe as I grumble under my breath. What the hell, I'm talking to myself again, at least I'm not answering myself.

I get up, look Sassy in the eyes and tell her enough of that shit, as I take her and let her outside in the backyard. I fill her bowls with food and water. I go to the bathroom jump in the shower and am back out in seven minutes. I dry off and put on my robe. I let Sassy in and go make my first cup of *Kafes*. I live for my

Kafes. I do not function without it. As I am taking my first sip, the phone rings. Ahhh, *I mama kai o papas calling.*

Thirty minutes later I hang up with my parents, promising I will be over in two weeks. I know next Friday I am going to that recital. The following Saturday, Debbie and I are going to the clubhouse to see Trent and the rest of the guys. They are having a family cookout. Trent called asking us to come down for it. I am so excited because we don't get to see him much. He needs to find himself a good woman, one that will put up with him that is.

I am out on my back porch with my *Kafes* and a book by Erin Trejo trying to get it read before Jax gets here. He called and said he was running about two hours behind, and so I thought this would give me enough time to get it finished. She is one of my top twelve favorite authors.

I just finish, when I hear him pull up and I'm still in my robe. "Shit, shit, shit," I say repeatedly. I run in the back door with my book and cup as he's knocking on the front door. I get to the door and open it for him. He looks at me with a heated look, scanning me from top to bottom. My mouth forms an 'O' as my breathing picks up.

He advances, and my feet are rooted in one spot. He is standing in front of me as he stares into my eyes and then looks at what's in my hands. He grins even more and takes it from my hand as he skims the pages. He asks me, "Did it make you hot and bothered, beautiful?" He sets it down and puts his hands around me, grabbing my ass and squeezing it like it's a piece of fruit, checking to make sure it's ripe enough. He leans in placing his lips on my lips and slowly sweeps his tongue on my lip wanting in. We are mating our tongues like we're having sex, and it is hot. He still has a slight hint of mint in his mouth. He attacks my neck and runs his mouth up to my ear, gently blowing in it. Man, that drives me out of my mind. I feel lightheaded, all hot and *bothered*. My pussy is wet, the wetness going down the inside of my leg. Jesus Almighty, I am going to need another shower. He lifts me, and heads down the hallway. He enters my bedroom, tells Sassy, "No, out." He shuts and locks the door to the bedroom. He sets me down with a bounce in the middle of the bed, sits and starts to take off his boots and jeans. He stands back up to pull them down the rest of the way, ripping off the bedcovers as he does it. Jax looks me in the eye and says, "If you don't want this tell me now." He takes a deep breath, "I don't know if I can stop once I start, I want you that badly. This is your last chance, once I fuck you, you are mine and I don't share."

"I don't share either." I moan. "Kiss me," I whisper. He leans back in, lips almost on mine, and the doorbell rings, and rings. I look at Jax, he looks at me and I see his mouth snap shut—*hard*.

"Your place is like fucking grand central station with trains coming and going at all hours. I can't believe this."

He gets up and I'm scrambling to get to the door. The doorbell keeps ringing.

I open the door. "Hi Dad, Mom. What are you doing here?" I mumble. "Did I forget lunch or something?" I ask innocently.

"We wanted to know if you would like to go to Nashville with us today?" they ask at the same time.

"Sorry, but I have plans for the day. Maybe the next time."

"Sure, honey, sure," my daddy whispers as he gives me a hug.

I keep praying Jax stays in the bedroom until they leave.

Mom leans in and gives me a hug and whispers in my ear, "Get back to your young man, honey." My jaw drops as they turn to leave. Mom looks back and winks at me.

I go back in and lock the door. I can't believe this shit. Only me.

CHAPTER FIVE

"I'm so sorry for the interruption. My family is always popping by but usually they call first. Are you okay? What's wrong?" I ask him.

"I would have loved to have met your parents. Maybe next time," he replies while looking away from me.

"Jax, I am so sorry. I didn't even think. Please forgive me," I say with a sorrowful look in my eyes as I grab onto his arm and go to face him so he knows I mean this. I kind of freeze for a minute, thinking to earlier when Jax came in. I am almost positive I locked the front door. He came in without me letting him in. I go to ask him about it when I glance at him and he is nodding his head, but it looks like he has so much more on his mind. I can't make him talk to me.

"You are so beautiful," he tells me. He keeps looking with his eyes roving all over my face. He bends down, and so softly kisses me again. He presses his face into the crook on my neck and keeps kissing me all over. "I could so fall for you," he states. "Let's go take a quick shower." I follow behind grabbing a couple of towels and a washcloth. He adjusts the shower and kisses me again while we wait for it to warm.

I do feel a little self-conscious because I have never showered with a man before, and I am a little spooked too. He notices my reluctance. "I haven't ever taken a shower with anyone," I tell him in one long breath.

"It's okay, honey. If you want to stop, we will. It's up to you. No pressure."

"I want to. I'm just a little nervous," I tell him as I step up into the shower.

We wash each other. I wash his hair and beard too. I love his beard. He takes the shampoo after rinsing the soap out of his hair, and lathers mine, rubbing it up to a nice thick lather. I rinse it out, and he turns off the water and we get ready to get out. We dry off and he gets re-dressed, while I get underwear and a bra out of my dresser. My under clothes are gray with a little pink on them, silky and smooth in texture. He whistles as I finish pulling them up my legs. I grab some shorts and tee shirt out of my closet. He heads out of the bedroom and grabs Sassy, talking to her. He tells her she is such a good baby and puts her out the back door. I go into the kitchen and grab a bottle of water. He takes the bottle and takes a drink out of it. "I can grab you one if you want?" I tell him. He smiles and tells me no.

He hugs me and grabs my butt like it's a piece of fruit again. I grin and shake my head at him. He tells me that his sister called while I was getting dressed and wants him to come by to help with his nephew, Jake, today for a few, and he wants me to go with him. "I would love to go with you," I tell him. He then says I need to get pants on with boots if I have them. He rode his motorcycle. I am dancing and jumping up and down in my mind. He grins. "You like motorcycles I take it?"

"Ummm... Yes, I do, as a matter of fact. What time?" I ask.

"Now beautiful, it's after two and we're supposed to be there by three or so," he tells me.

I go back and change into a pair of jeans and get socks and put my boots on. I have a pair of Harley boots for when I ride with Trent. I come out of the bedroom ready to go. Jax has brought in Sassy, made sure she has water and we are ready to leave. I go out the door with Jax behind me and shit, look at that bike. "Nice ride," I tell him.

"It's a 2016 Harley Fatboy. I had always wanted one, so I got it and use it a lot in the summer," he responds.

He looks at me and smiles, reaches and grabs my hand. As I'm walking down the sidewalk, Mrs. Franks leans over her railing waving her arms and wanting to know when she will get more cookies.

I look at her and tell her, "Never, not in a million years."

She laughs again at me and hollers out to Jax, "Hey, Hottie, want to get lucky?" I duck my head laughing. Jax just stares at her.

"I am a one-woman kinda man." I laugh out so loud, his face turns cherry red.

"What woman, you mean Ria? She don't know how to keep a hunka burning love like you happy. Come on over here honey bun. I can show you what a real woman can do."

By this time, I almost pee my panties, I'm laughing so hard. Jax just shakes his head, getting on his bike and starts it. He hands me a helmet, and asks me, "Are all your neighbors like her?"

"She is kind of special," I inform him. "She's been like that for as long as I have lived here."

"How old is she?

"About seventy-six years old. No close family near here. She lost her husband twenty years ago. She is loved by all in the neighborhood and we keep an eye on her for her granddaughter that lives about two hours away. She comes up about every two months." I get on the bike and we head out. It appears his sister lives in Evansville, close to his parents.

The weather is warm, in the high eighties. He jumps onto the parkway heading toward the strip. We pass a bunch of motorcycles, so I guess we all have the same idea today. As we pass the Audubon State Park, I see a lot of vehicles going in. *They must be having some sort of an event,* I think to myself. We get to the twin bridges, and of course need to slow some because of the construction.

I look over and see the tugboats and barges coming from both directions. I love to look at the Ohio River. I can see the sun glisten over the water, and it looks calm today. Jax swerves in the roadway and I clutch him harder around the waist. He looks back at me and I can see him grinning at me. I put my chin on his shoulder and tell him, "You didn't have to do that. All you had to do was tap my hand or leg." He, of course, runs his hand up and down my leg. He is dangerous. It takes about fifteen more minutes to get to his sister's house, but about a block away he waves at a man in a yard. I also see his blue Charger in the yard, or what looks like it.

We get to his sister's and I ask him if that's where he lives. He tells me that's where his parents live. I ask about his car, and he tells me that it's actually his brother Toby's. His sister comes out the front door with the two kids. He introduces me to them. She gives Jax a big hug and a kiss on the cheek.

The kids had run out and were climbing up his back. They are both so cute. Lacy looks like her mom, and the little boy Jake must look like his daddy. Cassie comes over and gives me a hug as well and tells me she is happy to meet me finally. We go into the house. Cassie takes me on a tour of the house, it's big. It's a beautiful home, with three levels. Kitchen and living room on the middle level. The bottom has a room that has a television with a small family room type setting. The laundry room has a door that leads to a one-car garage. The upstairs has three bedrooms with two bathrooms. The kitchen has a door that leads out to the back deck. Outside there is a pool and area to sunbathe. Cassie asks, "Would you like anything to drink?"

"That would be great," I tell her.

"I have beer, soda, water, or coffee," she tells me.

"Water sounds great. Thank you," I tell her.

"So, what do you do?" she asks me.

"I own my own salon. I've done hair since I've been twenty. I bought my salon a little over two years ago, with a loan from my parents. Since then, I have paid back the loan and it's all mine," I tell her. She asks where it's located and the name of the salon.

"*Unique Styles*, ever heard of it?" I ask her quizzically.

She tells me she has heard good things about the salon. I tell her thank you. Jax is with the kids and we continue to talk. She asks me if I know anything of Jax's previous relationship just as he comes up the last step from downstairs. He is furious; I can see it in his face.

"Cassie you need to butt out, but yes she knows. It's one of the very first things we discussed. You and Toby need to butt out and I'm not telling either one of you again," he tells her.

"By the way, what did you need me for today?" he asks her.

There is a pause, before she answers, "Well, the family wanted to meet Ria, so I told everyone to come over for a cookout. When you and I had talked earlier this week, I could tell there was something different about her. I could tell by the tone of your voice that she was special to you."

Oh, oh, I think to myself. He doesn't look very happy. "How did they find out?" he asks. He has his eyebrows raised. She doesn't say a word. He looks at me, grabs my hand, and tells his sister goodbye.

"Jax, Toby and I both told Mom and Dad about her. They overheard us talking about it. Please, they just wanted to meet her."

"Jax…" I'm trying to get him to slow down. His sister has tears in her eyes. "Jax," I say louder. He stops and turns. I put my arms around him and tell him I know he's upset. I kind of pick his brain, to find out his frame of mind. I want to know why he's so upset. "Tell me what's going on," I ask him. He tells me that they need to butt out of his relationships, that he is a full-grown man. I tell him I understand, that if he really doesn't want me to meet his parents that I won't say another word.

"It's not that I don't want you to meet them, I just don't want them to interfere in my relationship with you," he tells me.

"I honestly don't think that, that is what this is about. I think they are truly worried about you. I am assuming that they just want to make sure you're okay and see who I am too. I really don't mind Jax," I tell him with a kiss.

He kisses me back, turns around and tells his sister that he loves her, but they need to back off. He also tells her he had planned on introducing us in a couple of weeks. He continues to look at her as she twists her hands together nervously.

"What's for supper?" he asks finally.

"Well you and Daddy are cooking on the grill. Burgers and brats and Mom made her potato salad. I made a pan of baked beans that are in the oven now. I also made a red velvet cake," she states with tears in her eyes.

He looks at me, hugs me, and whispers in my ear, "Mine," with this unexplainable look.

I look at him with a shine in my eyes as I stare into his. "Yours," I tell him.

The doorbell rings, and in comes Toby as well as an elder Jax and a younger Cassie. They can't deny these kids. Jax looks like his daddy. A dead ringer picked out of his daddy's ass. No way to deny that parentage. They come in and give Cassie and the kids hugs. The kids take off and go back downstairs to the family room.

"Nice to see you again," Toby says.

"Hi Toby," I reply.

Jax gives his parents a hug, and his mom a kiss.

"Mom, Dad, this here is my girlfriend Ria. Her real name is Katarina. Ria these are my parents, Stewart and Eva." I go to reach to shake their hands and they both give me hugs, as I stiffen a second before I remember I'm safe. I don't like for others to get in my space if I don't know them. I am trying to get better with this, but it's a work in progress my counselor said.

"It's so nice to meet you, dear," Eva says.

"You sure are a pretty little thing," his dad says.

I smile and blush at the same time. His mom yells at his Dad. "Stu, not now. You just met her. Why do you do this you big flirt?"

"Thank you, Mr. Rawlings," I tell him.

Cassie tells Jax and Stewart that the patties are made, and she has the charcoal hot. Toby goes into the kitchen and grabs a few beers as they head outside. Cassie, Eva and I head out and bring in the items from the cars. We get everything prepped—tomatoes, lettuce and onions. We set the table that seats ten people. I grab a beer for us girls to drink and we head outside to sit and chat while we wait. The guys are gathered around flipping the burgers. They add the brats soon after. Jax heads my way, reaches down and gives me a kiss, then continues into the house. He hollers out and wants to know if anyone else needs a beer. We all decline.

Dinner is a loud and rambunctious affair. I have had such a great time ribbing Toby and talking with his parents. They are so fun, and my smartass tendencies come out a little. Not a lot, just a little. I don't want to scare them too much.

It's getting later, we have played board games with the kids. We have everything taken care of and it's time for us to leave. We give everyone a hug and I get a big kiss from the two kids. They are great. Lacy asks me to come to her recital this next Friday for the fundraiser. Jax tells her he won't get off in time, but I interrupt and let her know I will be there with my mom. She jumps up and down so excited. Jax looks at me and smiles. We get on the bike and head back over the twin bridges. I have my arms wrapped up tight around his waist, with the wind blowing in our faces. We get to my place. Jax unlocks the door and we go into the house. Sassy is jumping all around, up and under my feet. I see she had an accident, so I get it cleaned while Jax lets her outside. I am at the sink washing my hands when he comes up behind me placing his lips to my neck. I turn around in his arms and open my mouth under his lips. I love his lips. Sassy can be heard in the background scratching at the screen door. We let her in and turn on the tv. I ask Jax if he has to go home, and he tells me he does but he would be back tomorrow night to spend the night. We watch tv for about two hours and he gets up to go home. We have talked for most of the evening, just about mundane things. I walk him to the door and tell him goodnight. He backs out of the doorway as he looks at me. As he leaves, he waves. I have the door open and I am looking as he drives off down the roadway. I get chills down my back and feel as if someone is staring at me. I look around and don't see a thing. I close the door and lock up everything tight for the night. Windows and doors. I shut the shades in the living room, and holler at Sassy, letting her know it's time to get ready for bed.

CHAPTER SIX

Jax had come back on Sunday night, late after leaving. He called about one in the morning, standing on my front porch, and told me to open the door. He told me he just kept tossing and turning thinking of me, so he got some clothes for tomorrow and came back. We didn't do anything but sleep, and it was so nice to be held in his strong arms. I wake up in the middle of the night from a nightmare. I startle the hell out of him. I wouldn't tell him what it was about. He did hold me tighter and talked to me until I fell back asleep though, which I'm never able to do after one.

It's now Friday and I haven't seen Jax since Tuesday morning. We have both been extremely busy this week, but we have talked with each other every night for hours on end, from what we like to eat to some of our dislikes. The phone sex was unbelievable, and it's more freeing than anything in the world. I have the recital I'm going to tonight; Mom and Eva will meet each other too. I finally told my parents I'm dating someone and that it seems serious. My dad asked me if he was the one. I told him I fell fast and hard just like he said I would. I told him that we would be over soon so that I could introduce them to each other.

I need to finish cleaning up the salon and office and go home and clean up. I can't wait to meet some of the authors that may be there tonight, secretly of course. Jordan Marie, I have met in person at another event I attended on the down low, with Debbie. Dragon is the man… Mmmmm. One of these days I will have to come clean with my mom and Sophia too. The office is the last to be straightened up. I get done and holler at the girls on my way out the door. I will see Alexis in the morning.

I finally arrive at the venue for the dance recital and see Mom waiting on me, along with Debbie.

"Hey, Mom," I greet her as I kiss her. "I sure have missed you."

"Hi, honey," she responds as she gives me a hug. "You know where the house is," my Mom says, as I look at her and grin with that smirky-ass smile.

I look over and grin at Debbie. "Hey, bitch. What are you doing here?" She cackles at me. "I'm the good daughter. I went and picked up Mom. I was going to take her out for dinner and she insisted I eat dinner with her and Dad." Biting her lip trying to not laugh, she snorts instead.

"What time did you go over?" I ask her with my arms crossed.

"Well about four-ish or so," she replies with a snort. I shake my head at her. She eats there more than I do. She puts her arm through mine and I walk beside Mom on the way in.

We're walking down the carpeted corridor to the inside of the venues staging area, when Lacy sees me first. Screaming and running, she jumps into my arms. Cassie isn't far behind. I look at Cassie as she comes closer with a smile on my face. She walks up and gives me a hug. "Cassie this is my mom, Libby, and my best friend, Debbie. This here is Jax's sister Cassie and niece Lacy."

I'm looking around and see Eva walking our way. Eva walks up and gives me a hug and a kiss on the cheek. I introduce her as well. "You have a lovely daughter, Libby," Eva tells my mom as I blush a little.

We head inside, and I notice Mom and Eva talking as they walk side by side. It's about thirty minutes before the recital starts. I am so excited. Cassie and Lacy part from us as we enter the theater, we go to the left of the stage, and look for where there may be some empty seats. There aren't many left. Debbie asks me if Jax is coming and I shake my head no and tell her that he had a client and didn't think he would be done in time.

Just about the time we head down to our seats, I see my daddy coming in the side door. I smile really big. He walks up to Mom and she introduces him to Eva. I look down at the stage and see Stewart get up out of his seat as he makes his way toward us. Daddy comes and gives us girls a hug. "How's my baby doing? Your man going to be here?" he whispers. I shake my head no. I look my daddy in his eyes, and they sparkle with mischief. "Daddy, behave yourself," I tell him with a straight face trying not to laugh.

Introductions are made again. Stewart comes and gives me a hug. "Hey, beautiful," he says with a smile on his face. His eyes have crinkles at the side, a lot of them. He is a happy man. Just about that time I feel arms go around me and I jump, with an intake of breath.

I look over my shoulders and there is my dream man. I smile as I turn around in his arms. He leans down and gives me a big open mouth kiss. I look up and smile. "This is a really nice surprise. Why didn't you call me?" I ask him.

"I wasn't sure I could get off in time, honey, and I had someone drop me off. Can you give me a ride after?" he asks me. I nod my head, and he smiles real big. I turn or try to and introduce him to my parents. He bends to the side of me with his arm still around me and gives my momma a hug. He thrusts out his hand and shakes my daddy's hand. "It's nice to meet you both," he tells them.

My daddy looks at Jax, seriously looks at him, and asks him when we're getting married. My jaw drops as I sputter. Mom slaps Dad, then they start their banter with one another. I look at his parents and they're grinning, then bend over laughing. I look at Debbie and roll my eyes skyward. I look at Jax with such a serious expression. My lips are clenched, and I mutter, "I have no idea of who they are. I found them under a cabbage patch."

He bends down with a crease between his eyes. "We will be married before it's all said and done." His lips descend as fast as a hornet on a mission of stinging my ass.

After the recital we all decide to head out for a late dinner, although my parents and Debbie have eaten, they follow along for dessert and coffee. Lacy grabs my hand and wants to ride with me and her uncle Jax to the restaurant. Her uncle tells her it's up to me and of course I say yes. She is such a jovial spirit.

We are sitting in the local pizza parlor, the whole crew. All except Jake who is spending the evening with a friend. It has gotten loud and rambunctious in here. I had such a great time. Jax has had my hand in his for almost the entire night. He keeps staring at me.

I look at him and ask, "What?" He shakes his head and says nothing. "It's getting late and I have to be at the shop in the morning by nine." I tell him.

"I am going to have to get ready and go."

"Gonna take you home beautiful," he says with a whisper.

I nod okay. I get up and let everyone know, I need to leave.

"Lacy, thank you for inviting me to the recital. I had a great time and you are such a fantastic dancer. I hope you invite me to more," I say to her.

She nods. "Mommy you need to give Auntie Ria my dance schedule. She wants to come and watch. She said so," Lacy says with a little yell.

They all stand for a round of hugs and kisses, and we say good-night. Daddy hollers out, "You make sure she gets home safe, Jax."

Jax turns and nods. "Yes sir, I will."

He follows me out the front door, both hands on my lower back close to my ass. I love his hands. So big and strong. I feel so safe with him. He opens the car door for me and shuts it after I take a seat. A lot of men don't do that anymore. Chivalry is dead. We make small chit-chat on the way home. I was so happy he showed up.

"How was work today by the way?" I ask.

"It was great. I got it all done, added a couple small extra tattoos in and still was able to meet up with you on time," he says this with a devilish leer on his face.

We get to my house and I step out of my car. We head in the front door and I know I had locked it when I left. I know I did. I need to call Trent and let him know. The first thing that happens is my baby Sassy runs and starts scratching Jax's leg wanting up. He picks her up and puts her outside. He grabs me and we land on the couch. He is between my legs, his shirt coming off when there's a knock on the door.

"You have got to be fucking joking right now," he says with

disbelief. I look down and grab my shirt that he had helped me take off after we landed on the couch. I look downward, cussing under my breath as they continue to knock. It's late by anyone's standards. Who in the hell could it be? Jax stalks over to the door and jerks it open. There stands Pete. I turn pink in the face behind Jax. "Officer is there a problem?" Jax says obnoxiously.

Pete raises his eyebrows with arrogance, as he looks Jax up and down. "Nope," he says with a popping sound. I look at Pete and roll my eyes at him. Amusing, he's not tonight.

"Pete, did you need something?" I ask in an exasperated voice.

"Just checking up and making sure you are okay, Sis," he says with a witty voice. "Did I interrupt something, Sis?" he asks with a comical smile on his face.

"Not a damn thing you jackass," I reply with venom in my voice. "You know one of these days you will get yours, you know that don't you?" I tell him.

"Yeah, yeah. I've heard those promises for a few years." He laughs.

Jax has had enough. He pushes him out the door, slams it shut and mutters, "Cockblocker."

I can hear Pete walking away, all the while he's laughing like a loon. Jax stomps to the back door and lets Sassy in and tells her to go to bed. She looks at him and climbs up on the couch and puts her head on top of her paws. He takes my hand, before turning off the lights as we go down the hallway to the bedroom. He tells me it's warm, and I go to turn the air on. He tells me to just leave it off and he will open the windows in the bedroom. I freeze and tell him I would rather he just keep them locked. "I sleep better with the air on," I tell him.

He looks at me kind of strange, but I don't say anything else. I go and turn it on for him. I also check and make sure the doors are locked, again. I go back down the hallway and hear water running in the shower. I strip as I make my way into the bathroom. I open the door and he looks at me, grabs my hand and pulls me in. He takes my loofah bath sponge and puts my favorite scent of fresh linen on it as he lathers it up.

"I have missed you so much this week, Ria. I have missed your beautiful smile and body. Especially your body. Nice and round in all the right places. Perky titties," he remarks as he starts washing them.

"I have missed you so much, Jax. I wish you would have had time to come over this week," I state, as I take a washcloth, add soap and start to wash him.

He takes his hands and runs them over my body feverishly, kneading as he goes along. I can hear his breath catch as I start washing his penis. It's long with nice veins going through to the head of his cock. It jerks in my hand as he groans out loud like he's in pain.

I know I haven't hurt him, so I think he likes it. I haven't ever given a blowjob, but I so want to suck on his cock. I see a small drop of pre-cum on the tip of his shaft. I kneel down on my knees as I start licking from his balls up to the tip of his dick. I lean in more and start running my mouth over the tip. I go a little further and he groans out, "Fuck, that feels so good, beautiful." He takes his hand and runs it up my neck and grabs my hair, not hard, just tugging to let me know he likes what I'm doing to him. I am taking it as far as I can when I gag just a little. "Slower baby," he tells me. He moves his hips in short jerky movements and tells me to stop.

I don't want to and continue to kiss, lick and suck on his dick. I love the feel of it in my hands. I can feel it start to jerk a little. "Stop, beautiful, or I'm gonna come in that sweet mouth of yours." I moan as I continue, and he grabs my head as he starts to pound more into my mouth. I have spit coming out the side of my mouth and I can't stop. I am bringing him pleasure. I hear him moan and then start to roar out that he's coming. He pulses inside my mouth for what feels like forever. I keep trying to swallow what he's given me, but some leaks out the side and onto my lips. He is looking at me with a such an expression of lust. His cock is still semi-hard, and he picks me up off the floor of the shower. He takes his thumb and wipes it across my lip and stuffs it in my mouth, and I suck and lick it.

"You missed some," he says with a sensual edge to his voice. He embraces me. I wrap my arms around him and kiss his chest. I stare up at him through my eyelashes. He finishes washing us. I try to help, and I'm told no, with a rough voice.

I'm toweling off when I hear the phone ring. Jax looks at me with an incredible expression on his face.

"We are staying at my place from now on," he states. "This is ridiculous," he says with exasperation. I go to answer, and he jerks the phone up.

"Hello, who is this?" Shaking his head, he hands the phone over to me. I look at him, my eyebrows raised wondering who the hell it is.

"Hey, dearie," I hear.

"Mrs. Franks, are you okay?" I ask worriedly.

"I just wanted to make sure you were okay dearie with the police being there earlier. You didn't have problems with your hunka hunka man, did you?" she asks me with a humorous tone to her voice.

I lift the phone away from my ear, just absolutely at a loss for words at this point. I look at Jax. He's sitting on the side of the bed naked, elbows on his knees, head bent over with his hands on his head, pulling on his hair.

"Mrs. Franks, it's one o'clock in the morning. What in the world are you doing, don't you ever sleep?" I ask her as I plop down next to Jax.

"Well, dearie, I was worried," she tells me laughing.

She's laughing and I'm at a loss for words for a minute.

Then I'm on the crazy train.

"Are you out of your *ever-loving* mind, Mrs. Franks? Listen to me. Unless the place is on fire or the door is wide open, don't be calling knowing I have company, you *hear me*? Why would you wait until now to call anyway?" I sputter with a yell.

"I tried calling two times. You didn't answer," she says cackling.

"I was taking a shower Mrs. Franks. It's what you do before you go to bed," I say.

"Musta been an awful long shower." She pauses. "Did you get some shower sex, honey?" she asks laughing out loud.

"Mrs. Franks, I am calling your granddaughter tomorrow. This is completely out of hand. You understand me? Now I gotta go, we will talk tomorrow when I get home from work." With each syllable getting a decibel higher, I go to slam the phone down when I hear her next statement. *I want to scream to the high-heavens I think.*

"So, I guess I need to call them police officers and tell them I got ahold of you and you are A-Okay? I'll just tell them you were having wild monkey sex in the shower with your man and didn't hear the phone." She stops speaking for a minute then says, "That okay?" as she laughs so hard, she can't catch her breath.

"You better not have, Mrs. Franks," I say just as the front door-bell rings. I slam the phone down, and stomp toward the front of the house. I have Jax chasing after me trying to pull up his jeans, going commando.

"You better not touch that fuckin door, beautiful, I will spank that ass," he roars so loud that Sassy starts barking and jumping around.

"It's the cops, Jax," I reply. "Mrs. Franks called them."

"I don't care who called them. You answer that door I will spank that ass," he repeats.

"Look down," he shouts.

"Oh. My. God. I'm naked… Oh, my God, I don't have any clothes on, Jax," I screech as loud as someone running their fingernails over a chalkboard.

I go running to the back of the house, slip on my robe and hear Jax and Pete arguing. I run back to the front door.

"Shut up, the both of you!" I yell.

"Pete you knew nothing was wrong. You knew he was here. Go home. Go fight the law elsewhere. I'm done. I'm going to kick her ass tomorrow, you understand me. You better not respond. You hear me. You better not respond to any calls for her house unless they're from me," I tell him with a riled breathy tone.

He looks at me and grins as he walks away from the front door. Sassy is still barking, Jax is pissed, I am pissed. Jax slams the door and locks it. He turns around and looks at me.

"Any other fucking crazies in your life?" he asks.

"Yeah, my whole family," I smart off. "Jax honey, I'm tired. Everyone has wore me the fuck out and I want to go to bed. They aren't doing this just because you're here. I deal with this shit all the time," I inform him with a grin.

"God save me," he says grinning.

He takes my hand and we go to bed. I curl up next to him with my head on his shoulder, my arm wrapped around his middle. "Night, handsome," I say drowsily.

"Night, beautiful," he replies as he tightens his arm around me. He links his fingers with mine on his.

CHAPTER SEVEN

SEVEN DAYS LATER

"Shit... Shit... Shit..." I mutter as I try to gather my bags, dog food, crate and toys for Sassy. The doorbell rings and it's my mom coming to get her and her things for the weekend.

I go to unlock the door for her. "Hey mom, I have Sassy's things all ready to go. I don't know what time I'll be home on Monday. We're staying for the whole weekend," I tell her.

"We love having her, honey. I'll bring her home on Tuesday for you. That way you can take your time getting back," she tells me. She leans in and gives me a hug and a kiss on the cheek.

"How are you doing, sweetheart? I like Jax, he seems to have it together and he really likes you," she states.

"I'm doing okay. I really like him. I think he could be the one, but after the last fiasco I'm not sure I trust my own judgement." As I look her in the eyes, I tell her this, with a forlorn look on my face.

"Have you been going to any meetings?" she asks.

"I've been going to some noon meetings during my lunch breaks. Actually, a lot of them. It's one of the reasons I want to go to the clubhouse this weekend. I need to talk to Trent. He understands me," I tell her with tears in my eyes.

"Have you told Jax anything?" she asks with a small gloomy look in her gaze. I shake my head no. I drift back in time for a minute.

"No, Mom. I'm just not ready. I want this so much. He is so good to me. He calls me every night. I don't want him to look at me any differently. I'm afraid if I say anything it will change. I'm not ready for that," I state in a low whisper. We have a quick drink as I wait on Debbie to get here. We have already loaded all of Sassy's things into mom's car.

Debbie pulls in and honks her horn. I start locking up the doors and making sure the windows are secure. I grab my bag and set it on the porch as I shut the door. I take my keys and lock the deadbolt too.

Mom is backing out and hollers for us girls to be careful and to have a good time. We decide to take my car which is fine by me. We load it up and I head on down 60 and hit the back street to downtown Henderson. I'm going to see Jax before we go out of town.

Walking in the front door of the shop, I see Toby coming in through the back door with a box. He smiles and waves at me as he sets it down on the cabinet in the back. He comes up front and gives me a hug. I smile and ask if Jax is busy.

Toby hollers and Jax comes out of his room. He smiles when he sees me. He sweeps in and lip-lock city is on. Man, he has a set of lips and a tongue that need a warning label, hot... *sizzling hot*.

With his arms wrapped around me, he lifts me up off the floor and twirls me around and around.

"Hey, big man, slow down before I get sick," I say with a grin.

"You get sick, you can stay home, and I'll take care of you. I am going to miss you," he says with his lips all puckered out in a pout.

I laugh and lean in to kiss him. "I am going to miss you too, so much," I whisper in his ear. I lay my head down on his shoulder and squeeze him tighter. "We're going to have to go. It's five now and it's about a two to two-and-a-half-hour ride there. Debbie has missed Trent and we're having dinner tonight with him."

He looks at me with such tenderness. "Be safe going and coming. I'll see you on Monday. Call me when you get there," he tells me.

He walks us out to my car. He blocks me in by the door, leans in and starts kissing my chest, my neck and he is hard. His dick is so hard, it makes me wet. We're both just nipping, licking, and sucking on each other when over a bullhorn we hear, "Break it up, the center of town is about to combust. Break it up you two." Pete starts laughing. Debbie is out of the car leaning over the top, face planted on the side of the car laughing like a loon. I start to shake and laugh as the people around us start to hoot and holler. Oh my God... It's happened again.

I look over at Pete, he has his phone out recording us. "What the hell are you doing Pete?" I snarl.

"Making a video for Mrs. Franks. She'll pay good money for this," he tells me, laughing.

Jax mutters, "For fuck's sake."

Debbie has been laughing so hard she runs back into the shop. "Where the hell are you going?" I ask her.

Laughingly she tells me, "I'm about to pee my panties."

This is unbelievable. Totally!

"Pete, I have had to put up with enough of your shit to last a lifetime. Your time will come. You hear me?" I tell him with a despicable hissing breath.

Jax's hands smooth over my back, my face planted right up on his chest under his chin. God, he smells so good. He always does. "Jax, honey, what kind of cologne do you use? It smells so damn *gooooodddd*," I tell him sniffing his neck and chest.

"Stop, Ria, unless you stay, and we go up to my place now," he growls.

Debbie is making her way back outside. I have been ignoring Pete and everyone that has stopped to watch the spectacle of our love life. Debbie gets in the car as Jax helps guide me to my seat behind the driver's wheel. I plop my ass down as I twist my legs in. He reaches down and gives me a kiss. "I sure am going to miss you, beautiful."

"I'm going to miss you too. Bye, honey," I tell him.

He closes the door and steps away as I start to back out. As I drive away, I wave with a smile on my face. Windows rolled down, "Pete, you're a *dick face*," I yell. I jump on the gas as we peel out down the road. I can see both Pete and Jax yelling and waving to slow down.

Debbie turns down the radio. "You okay Sis?" she asks me. I shake my head no. "I need to talk to Trent," I tell her. "I'm so scared of my feelings for him. I care so much for Jax, and I don't know what to do."

"Have you had sex with him yet?" she wants to know.

"No, we've fooled around and for a while I wasn't even thinking about things from our past, but lately things have been a little off. I have been freezing up, or the fucking phone rings, or *your* brother shows up. I can't catch a break. We're always inter-rupted, and I feel that that's a sign that we shouldn't be together. I just don't know anymore. Call me melodramatic, or the crazy one, but that's how I feel. I'm falling in love with him and I'm afraid to show too much emotion with him. I have had a few nightmares the last week or so, and it's freaking me out." I say all of this with tears running down my face and my heart is torn in two.

I pull into the gas station just before the parkway that leads south toward Nashville. We get out and go in and we each get a fountain soda and snacks for the road. I let Debbie take over driving. I'm a mess at this point. We talk about small things. I try not to discuss much of what's bothering me with her. She still to this day blames herself for this. I don't know why. She won't talk about it to me or anyone else. I know she's still in counseling. She goes once a week to a place in Owensboro. I've told her I would go with her and she just flat out says *no.* She wouldn't see or talk to me for the longest time after I was found. It took about six months before I saw her. It took even longer for us to get back to our normal friendship. The way we once were before.

The day is beautiful, warm, and sunny with a slight breeze in the trees. The trees are still a nice vibrant green. In the next two months the weather will change from fall to winter type weather. I don't think we ever have too much of either spring or fall here in the Midwest. We go past parts of the interstate of 24 east and it has mountain rocks on both sides of the roadway. Music is blaring, and we listen to one of my all-time favorites *Devil Woman* on the radio.

The closer we get, the more traffic we come up on in Nashville. We hit 65 south and go up a few miles as we exit. It's a little built up but further on down the road more of the houses become a little more run down and scarcer. We pull up on the side road and head out about one mile when we see lots and lots of barbed wire fencing. It looks like a prison of sorts but it's the local MC club where Trent is a member. He's the vice president of the club. He's also not someone that will take any shit from anyone. He's my savior, my confidant, and my family's adopted son. Through and through my brother from another mother and father. I don't know what I would do without him. He has always been there for me. I know Pete knows, but he doesn't understand the way that Trent does. I need him to help me work through this shit in my head. Fast like.

We pull up to the gate and some guy we've never met is there at the door.

"You ladies lost?" he asks us.

"No, we're here to see Trent, you wanna open the gate?" says Debbie in a laughing way just to see what he does. I have a grin on my face. She has disrespected him. He scowls at us. He calls inside, and I watch the door to the clubhouse open. I see the president Garr come out the side door. He's looking and then sees me waving as Debbie is giving that boy shit. "Open the door, dickhead," she says. I am shaking my head. Garr gets to the gate and tells the prospect to open the gate; that we are family. He is to open it anytime he sees either one of us girls.

"Debbie don't be giving my boys shit either," he says with a smirk.

We pull in and park by the other cars across the way from the motorcycles.

Garr is walking our way when Debbie gets out, runs and jumps in his arms. I always thought that he and Debbie should hook up, but Trent would go batshit crazy if he thought anything was there on president's side. I honestly think there is, but they both deny it. He looks at her with defeated eyes sometimes. Like she's something he wants but knows he can never have.

I get out, grab my shit out of the back end as some of the other fellows come out. "Where's Trent?" I ask. Garr looks at me and tells me he had to go pick up a part for a car that is being worked on and will be back shortly.

"Come on up to the clubhouse girls. Bring your shit with you." The fellas take our things and proceed to put our stuff in one of the spare rooms for guests. We normally share a room. One of the nicer ones. It has two beds, a tv, a desk and two chairs. It also has a nice large bathroom inside for us to use—one we don't have to share with others.

We head toward the bar and Angie plops down our Diet Pepsi that we drink. Garr sits in the middle.

"How was your trip up ladies?" he asks us.

"Not too bad," replies Debbie.

"Good, good. Was wondering what time you all would be here. The Twinkies are cooking. Margie is in there telling them what to make us for dinner. You all hungry?" he asks.

"I am," Debbie states as I nod my head.

"A little," I reply, as I am looking at and around the seating area.

The place is done up in grays and more grays. Some are lighter, and some are darker. It has wooden beams across the ceiling that are black in color. They have about fifteen tables scattered throughout the area. Some hold four, and some six. A jukebox is on the wall close to the dance floor, if you want to call it that. Two bathrooms that are nice if they were actually clean, but usually they are nasty. To the left of the bar is the door to the kitchen and stock room. If you go to the right after leaving the bar going toward the kitchen there is a long hallway that actually leads to the rooms for club members. If you look past the bar on the right, you will see a door that has a short hallway that leads to the meeting room. That's where they hold 'church.' I love being here, and I feel safe *all* the time.

The doors don't even need to be locked. I can open the windows in my room here. Trent and the guys and the ol' ladies made it my safe place. I actually spent about three months here after the kidnapping because I didn't feel safe without him. While I was here, they taught me self-defense. Hard core self-defense. I'm considered a sharp-shooter, have a third-degree blackbelt which didn't happen overnight. My parents continued to take me at Trent's insistence. They taught me street fighting too. No one, not even Debbie, is aware of my ability of all of these. I take classes occasionally to keep my skills up. My mom and dad were so upset with the situation, but trusted Trent and the fellas to help me through it all. They hired a full-time counselor that stayed on-site for the time I was here. My parents would come down occasionally while I was here, but they understood it better when they noticed the difference in me.

As I sit here and reflect on where my life was and where I want it to go, I see Garr taking sneak peeks at Debbie. Oh, shit may hit the fan. I pray not. I honestly think that they would be good for one another. Even with the age difference, they complement one another. I also see a gleam in my bestie's eyes that I've never seen before. I will have to pick her brains soon. Like tonight...

CHAPTER EIGHT

It's going on six o'clock when I see Trent come through the door. He's talking with Speck. I sit back and watch as Debbie goes running and jumps in his arms. He gives her a huge hug and I see them talking to one another. He looks over after she says something, and she does too. They've been talking about me. He gives her another hug, tells Speck something and starts my way. I see Speck give Debbie a hug. I hear a deep grumble and look to my left, it's Garr with a pissed-off expression on his face. I lean down my face and say under my breath to Garr, that Trent is almost up on us and he needs to cool it. He looks over at me, stands up and walks toward the kitchen. Debbie sees him go and the smile on her face falls. I see tears well up and she goes off toward the kitchen too. I hear Debbie ask what room we are staying in and Margie tells her same as usual.

Trent finally arrives and leans in and gives me a really big hug, and I start to cry before he even says a word. I am shattered, and I haven't told him a thing. He draws me close with my head on his shoulder, whispering and telling me it will be okay. He tells

Angie to get me a shot of Jack, straight up. I laugh and blubber all over the front of him. My face and eyes are red-rimmed, splotchy, and swollen now. What a sight I must be. Angie sets two glasses down for each of us, with a beaming smile on her rosy little face.

I throw the first down and choke a little at first. It burns on the way down, but almost instantly warms the belly. I reach over for the second shot and do the same. It's much smoother this time going down and tastes that much better. Trent takes his thumbs and wipes my tears away. He smiles at me.

"Reason why you are packing heat, Sis?" he asks me with curiosity

"Food first then we will talk," I reply back with attitude.

"Dinner first, honey, then we'll hole up and we can talk," he tells me. I know that having dinner will be first. No matter what, it's going to happen this way. See, Trent is a take charge kind of guy. He just expects everyone to agree to what he wants.

"That's fine. I am a little hungry," I say with a half-smile.

"Care to tell me why Garr took off so fast?" he asks me with that infamous stare of his.

"I have no idea of what you're talking about," I tell him with an innocent look.

"Okay, we'll play it your way for now, but I saw you say something to him when he got up and left," he states.

I shrug my shoulders, and he takes his hand, squeezes my shoulder and steers me into the dining area. He looks around for Debbie and asks Margie if she's seen her. She tells him that she went to her room to clean up for dinner. I look at Trent and tell him I'll go get her for dinner. He nods okay.

I take off down the hallway and hear some arguing. I rush down looking behind me to make sure Trent isn't behind me. I go to enter our room and the door is locked. I bang on the door, and shout whisper loudly for them to open the door. It gets really quiet, and Debbie opens the door. I have my eyebrows raised and ask her if she knows what she's doing, especially with her brother down the hallway. Garr comes up behind her and pushes his way out, putting his cut back on. Both of them have swollen lips, hair standing on end. I just shake my head. I tell them both that he already asked me what was going on. I tell Garr, that I won't lie to Trent. He nods his head and tells me nothing was going on.

"Sure, if you say so, Pres. That's why your hair is a mess and your lips are all swollen and wet," I inform him with a hint of smartassism.

"Watch it," he tells me in a low voice. "This is my house. My club. You are a welcome guest, but you will watch how you talk to me."

I nod my head. "Understood."

I hear my cell going off with an incoming message. It's Jax. I smile, excuse myself to respond to his text.

I turn around and go sit in one of the chairs and text him back.

Jax: You make it okay Ria? Good trip?

Ria: I'm here. Got here about an hour ago. Just got to my room to put my things up. Leaving for dinner in a minute. What are you doing?

Jax: Just got done with my last appointment for the night. I miss you, beautiful. XOXO

Ria: I miss you too, handsome. I'll send you a message when we get back, although it may be a little later. That okay?

Jax: Great, anytime. Have fun, just not too much. Hugs beautiful

Ria: XOXOXO, talk later.

I'm sitting beside Trent and have just finished dinner. Margie and the girls sure can cook. There are about twenty of us tonight. Some get up and head toward the bar. Trent gets up and takes my hand. He heads toward the bar and asks for two and two. Angie places two shots and two beers on the bar top.

"Here, drink up, toots," he says.

I throw back the shot with a grimace, shivers run through my body as it travels down my throat into my belly. I pick up my beer and he grabs my hand and drags me slowly out the back door. I see Debbie sitting with the girls getting her drink on too.

"Hey kiddo what's going on?" he asks me.

"I've met someone, but I am so unsure of myself. Well, I wasn't at first, then some strange shit started happening. Doors being unlocked when I know I locked them. Sassy a little more crazy than normal. I feel like someone is watching me sometimes. I don't see anyone though. I don't trust my instincts. After Hedrick, I just..." I fade off while speaking.

"Honey, only you can decide if he's the one. Only you can decide if he's worth the effort. Only you can decide what to tell him. Keeping him in the dark though is not fair to him. Do you care for him?" he asks.

"More than anything. I think I'm falling in love with him," I sob out.

"Why are you crying then? As for the doors and such, you should have called me immediately. I will see about getting some monitors set up, okay?" he tells me.

"I don't know. I just don't know. I wake up sometimes reaching for him; some of the nightmares have come back. I am going to more meeting again."

"Have you had sex with him yet?"

"No… I want to. We've fooled around, but we have been interrupted a lot. Then all the shit with the doors and stuff, I am spooked. Then the infamous duo—the asshole Pete and Ms. Meddlesome Franks—keep interrupting us." I laugh with a sniffle. He places his arm around me and squeezes me to his side. He chuckles.

"I'm afraid if I can't follow through, he'll get mad like *jerk face* did."

"He wasn't a man. He was an abuser. You can do much better than that piece of shit and I done already told you that before. If he cares for you, he will help you get through this. Have you tried going back into counseling?" he asks.

"I have thought a lot about it lately. I have also been hitting about four to five meetings a week. I go on my lunch break so that I'm not out after dark by myself," I state while my head bounces up and down in an affirmative response. "I am better, I know I'm stronger too. We've spent the night together," I say.

"Really, and I'm just now hearing about this?" he mutters. "Damn Pete," he states. I look down with a smile on my face. *Ha. Ha*, I think to myself. Pete is in trouble now. I told him he would pay.

Angie is coming out the back door with two more beers and hands them to us. "Thanks, Angie," we both say at the same time. We look at each other and grin.

"Honestly, Trent, I have fallen in love with him. What if he can't handle my quirks about sex? I gave him a blowjob in the shower one night," I blurt this out so fast he spews his beer all over.

"Why did you tell me that, at that exact moment?" he growls.

"I had to say it. I felt like I had to. I need you to tell me this is real, that he is the one. At first I never even thought twice about not having sex with him. Since the unlocked doors and shit, I am more frazzled. I have taken to packing my gun with me everywhere I go now. I feel safe with you and you're the one I always come to. You are my safety net." I whisper so low he can barely hear me.

"Honey, I can't tell you that. I haven't even met the man. I can say that what I have been told he seems to be legit in his feelings toward you," he rumbles in that deep growly voice of his.

I go through the same feelings, just like the kidnapping happened yesterday. I know it's not the same, but I'm out of my element here. I remember how much weight I gained. Trying to make myself unattractive. I thought that if I was ugly, it never would have happened. I know that's not the case, but I had all these emotions and I didn't know what to do with them.

"Look, Sis, you'll never know unless you try and put yourself out there. I know you know how to defend yourself now. I taught you. I know you know how to shoot, I taught you. I know you know how to slice a person open. I even taught you that. I know you can poke a person's eye out. You have to decide if he's worth it. A man can't make up your mind for you. So, my question is, is he worth it?"

"I know, I want him. I'm just so torn. I know he's worth it, but is he going to think I am? He's been through some shit himself. His bitch of an ex aborted his baby and told him she had a miscarriage. Then, she screws his best friend. His ex-best friend called a while back and told Jax that he was sorry, and she did the same thing to him. The only difference is she was married to the best friend," I tell him.

"Right now, let's get you in the right frame of mind. Then we'll discuss your man," he says.

"Do you still cringe when someone tries to touch you?"

I shake my head no. "Although, sometimes I freeze up if it's a man."

"Do you still lock everything up tighter than a drum?" I nod my head. "Do you still binge eat?" I respond no. "You said you have had a couple of nightmares?" he asks.

"No, not in a long time," I reply.

"Still shy away from walking down the street?" he asks me while gazing into my eyes.

"It's getting better, or it was, now I feel like someone is watching me," I mutter. It is, it's not as bad as it was. I can go out and get my mail. I walk the streets in town if it's busy. I'm always looking around my surroundings when I'm out there. I am keeping myself safe.

I am still a bit of a mess. I was doing better and now I have this crap that keeps happening, I know I have come a long way. I just feel like I am getting trapped back where I was watching everything around me. My sexuality is more than it was for a long time. I wear clothes that complement my body. Not big and baggy like I wore for two years. I love myself and I am a strong and happy woman. I am not a dirty cunt or whore.

I was a virgin, and although I'm technically not one now, I still feel as if I'm a virgin. That was stolen from me. I should be able to give myself to a man I care about for the first time and still feel like it is the *first* time. I know Jax is the one for me. I love him. Now I need to see if he can understand what I have been through. I turn to Trent and with tears running down my face, I say, "He's the one, Trent." I pause for a moment. "Jax is my everything," I blurt out, with one of the happiest smiles ever.

Trent looks at me and smiles so big. "I know kiddo, I know. I'm glad you figured it out on your own. I just sat and listened and asked you questions like you were in therapy. I love you, kid. Don't ever doubt yourself. You may have been a victim, but you are now a survivor. Remember that," he tells me with a sheen in his eyes. We get up and head into the clubhouse. He asks me if I want another beer and I tell him I do. We grab one at the bar and head over to the couch and chairs section. They have a little area off of it with a tv and such mounted so that they can watch that together when they want. There are several people including Debbie. Garr, I notice was in the bar with a Twinkie in his lap.

Trent sits in the chair and pulls me onto his lap. He rubs my back and I get a few nasty looks from some of the Twinkies sitting by Debbie. I just grin at them. I can take them.

I turn toward Trent and whisper, "I'm pissing off the girls." He looks up and stares at them a second, looks at me and kisses me on my jaw.

"Oh, hell no. You can't pull me into your games, Trent. I have a man. I don't do this shit," I hiss.

"He isn't here and it's a joke. They've been all over my ass, and I don't want no ol' lady. Women are a pain in my ass. You, lil sis, are my protector for the weekend," he says with a shit-eating grin on his face.

I just sit there, and we give each other shit for the rest of the night as I continue to get evil eyes from the Twinkies. Trent is having a grand old time at my expense. That old saying *what goes around comes around*. He will get his. Just like Pete is getting his soon. I *smile*.

◇

It's Monday and we are loading up the car. I have missed Jax and Sassy a lot over the weekend. Trent and I talked a lot. I feel somewhat better and it looks like I'll be having a long talk with my man, Jax, tomorrow night. I'm taking Wednesday off work, so he's coming over for dinner. I told him it would be later when I got in and to just hold off until then to come over.

CHAPTER NINE

I arrive at work at eight. I have some paperwork I want to get caught up on. My first appointment isn't until ten. I want to get this done so I don't feel guilty for taking tomorrow off work. I have a lot on my mind and I just keep replaying what I want to say. Only Alexis knows what happened so long ago, she was here one day while something triggered a meltdown. She called my mom and she rushed right over. I love my little shop and my family of workers. We seem to sync with each other with what we do. I'm better at color, Mary more toward perms and straightening of the hair. She is also the bomb at putting in extensions. Alexis really likes cutting hair but likes the nails and waxing too. I unlock the door and turn around and relock it behind me. I look around as I go and turn off the alarm to see if anything is out of place. It seems that with all the feeling and talking of that time, I am more on edge. I need to make sure to hit a meeting today. I'm excited and all twisted up on my insides. I go to my office and pull out receipts and such and start logging onto my computer. I grab a diet Pepsi out of my small refrigerator and get to work with inputting information for taxes. I have quarterly taxes coming up soon. I am so engrossed with doing my work when the girls pop their head in the door, it scares the bejesus out of me. I just jump in my seat and scream. My heart is pounding, and Alexis says sorry really loud to get my attention. I tell her I'm okay and to give me a minute.

I walk out to the break room and the girls are putting their things up. They all turn and ask how my weekend was. All because they think Trent is a *hottie*. I have never in my life seen so many females go ga-ga over a male. He is cute but Jax is much *hotter*.

I fill them in, and they set out to open the shop while I head back into my office. I sit on my couch and lean back. I didn't sleep well last night and after that scare I am jumping out of my skin. I just sit there and let my mind wander about nothing. The next thing I know, I hear Alexis calling my name. She tells me my appointment is there and asks me if I am truly okay.

"Honestly, I don't know. My nerves are shot, and I didn't sleep well last night. I miss Jax and in the next sense I don't want to see him tonight. It's time we sat down and had a heart-to-heart. I'm going to a meeting today at lunch. That should help some. It normally does."

She looks at me and smiles. "Ria, he is crazy about you and you both will be okay. Take a deep breath, blow it into a balloon and let it all go."

I take out the imaginary balloon and blow it up. Then I release it. This is something I learned in therapy and the girls once asked me a long time ago what it meant. I just told them, that's what I do with my problems. I look at her and smile. We both head out to the front and I get to work on my first client. I have her color on when my next one walks in. I get her set up and start her color. Before I know it, I have both ladies done and I have thirty minutes before my meeting. I am cleaning my area up when Toby walks in.

"Hey Toby, what are you doing here?" I ask him.

"Need a trim if you have time, Ria." I nod my head yes, as he sits in my chair. I put on the cape and take him to wash his hair. While we are talking, he asks me about my weekend. I let him know that I had a good time and I'm glad to be home.

"Hey, can I ask you a question?" he asks as I start to cut his hair.

"Sure, whatcha want to know?" I say with an eyebrow raised.

"Debbie seeing anyone?" he asks in a lower voice.

"Debbie?" I repeat, with my eyes wide open.

"Yeah, Debbie, your best bud?" he says snappishly funny.

"Um, well not to my knowledge, why?" I retort.

"Because I think she's beautiful and I wanna ask her out, that's why, smartass," he says with a Cheshire grin.

I just roll my eyes at him. I finish cutting his hair and tell him twenty dollars. He looks at me, reaches back and hands me the money out of his wallet. I just grin at him.

"Can I have her number?" he asks.

"No, I will ask if I can give it to you though," I tell him with a laugh.

He shakes his head and mutters on his way to the door.

"You want to go have lunch?" he asks.

"Sorry, I have some errands I need to run today, Toby. Maybe next time?" He nods his head yes.

I holler at the girls as I sweep up Toby's hair that I'm leaving as soon as I get it done. I go get my purse and out the door I go. I get in my car and head to the meeting.

I walk in and there are about eight ladies here. I say hi and settle in for the hour. I tell them about me and what's going on. We all talk. They tell me that I need to put myself out there. Just take it one thing at a time. One of the ladies understands, she was where I am now a year ago in a new relationship. We don't use names out of the meeting. Most of us have all been in this same group for a few years. We do call and support one another over the phone if we need to. I'm asked if I can take the hotline for an extra night this next week and I assure them I can. I say my goodbyes and head out the door.

Things have been busy the rest of the afternoon, but I am in a better frame of mind. I am locking up when my phone rings. It's Jax.

"Hey, beautiful, I'm running about thirty minutes behind. That okay?" he asks me.

"Hey, handsome. That's fine, I'm just leaving the salon now and I'm stopping off at the grocery store. Any requests?" I ask him with a smile on my face.

"Yeah, can you pick me up a six pack of beer?"

"Sure, I can. That isn't a problem. I've missed you, a bunch."

"You know that's the first time you have said that, that it really sounds like you mean it. You've been distracted for a while. I've been worried," he states with a dejected voice.

"I know I have. I need to tell you some things tonight. I'm sorry you feel like I don't care. It's the opposite though. I love you, Jax. I want you to know that. Above all else that happens tonight, know that." I sob in distress. "I've got to go. I'll see you soon, handsome." I disconnect my phone and turn off the ringer. I turn back and make sure I have locked up tight.

I make it to the grocery store and decide it's going to be sloppy joes tonight with fries. Quick and easy. I get my groceries and check out and head home. It's overcast a little tonight. I hope it doesn't storm. I hate storms. The skies look wicked, blue and black hues and all the clouds are swirling.

I jump in my car and take off for home. I get there and remember to call my mom.

I dial her number and she answers on the second ring. "Mom, it's looking bad this way. You just want to keep Sassy another night and I can get her in the morning sometime?" I say. She responds that she'll keep her and bring her home on the way to her doctor's appointment. "That's fine, Mom. Love you. Talk to you tomorrow sometime. Okay?" We hang up. I look around as I grab my keys and groceries and I get out of my car. I just get a feeling that someone is watching. I bet it's Mrs. Franks again. I thought they would have stopped since I was in Tennessee. I unlock the door and turn around and relock it. I turn on some lights as I go into the kitchen. It's small but I love the granite counter tops and small island that sits there in the middle. The cabinets are a medium tone gray. Off-white with gray splatters in the flooring tiles and white granite counter tops. This is a small replica of what my dream kitchen would be when I get married. I wonder where Jax lives. I have never been there, but he keeps saying he's moving me in. I put up the few things I picked up, putting the beer in the fridge to keep it cold. I throw the ground beef in a skillet and turn the burner on low.

I head off to change clothes and come back out about three minutes later. I look over as I'm coming out of the hallway and think I see someone looking in the side window. I jump and let out a yelp. The bell rings. I go slowly to answer it. I look out the peep hole and it's Pete.

"Yes, Pete," I say opening the door. He looks amused and pissed. "Is there a problem?" I question with a grin.

"*Is there a problem?*" he snaps out with a foul attitude.

"I don't know, I asked you first, dickwad. You came here. I didn't come to your place." I sneer back at him with my nose up in the air.

He starts to come forward and I lock the front screen door on him. His mouth drops open. "Look you, big ape, I have plans tonight. Don't respond to Mrs. Franks unless she says someone is dying. Do not come to my door. Don't be calling my phone either, officer," I yell at him, the sound escalating louder with each word. "Now, is there a problem, Pete?" I ask again.

"You know you can be a real pain in my ass, Ria. I can't believe you told Trent. He is all over my ass. Now I have to try and control Mrs. Franks. That is almost impossible," he hisses at me.

I smirk. "You started it. I just finished it you green-eyed jackass."

He stomps his booted foot on the porch. You can actually see the steam coming out of his ears. He turns and storms off the porch to go to Mrs. Franks. He looks over his shoulder. I wave my fingers and mutter "Ta-ta." He knows what I said. I could see it in his eyes.

I shut and lock the door and run to the kitchen to make sure nothing burned. I put the fries on the pan and start the oven. I get the fine china out for dinner tonight, within our family that means paper plates. I have no desire to do the dishes. I just finish up dinner when I hear a knock at the door. It's not but a little after seven so I don't believe it's Jax. I go look through the keyhole and open the door.

CHAPTER TEN

I stare mesmerized with tears just flowing down my face. I start to sob uncontrollably and can't seem to stop. I have so much emotion running through me, and all I can say is, "I love you Jax. I love you so much." He looks at me bewildered with an uncertain look in his gaze. He goes to open the door and it's still locked.

"Open the door, beautiful. Open the door," he demands in a gruff voice.

I stretch my arm out with a shaking hand, my whole body seems to be trembling as I unlock the door. He has it open before my hand is off the lock and I fall forward into his arms. He wraps his arms around me, lifts me up, and closes the door locking it behind us.

"Hey, beautiful, what's wrong?" he asks as he wipes the tears off my face.

I just continue to sob, I can't talk. I shake my head as he continues to whisper in a crooning voice. I've held off for the last month, keeping all of this to myself. I should have discussed this with him before.

He hears the timer on the oven go off. He moves me to the couch, sets me down on it, and goes and turns off the oven and removes the fries. He comes back into the living room and sits beside me, picking me up and putting me in his lap. I am still a mess but slowly the water works slow down. He takes a Kleenex off the end table and mops my face.

"Are you going to tell me why you're crying and sobbing like this. Are you sick or something?" he asks me, worriedly.

I deny being sick with a quick shake of my head. My head is tilted while gazing into his beautiful brown eyes, my lips trembling.

"You're scaring me. What's wrong?" he asks while he still rubs my back.

As he continues to rub my back, I calm down even more. The constant feel of him helps with that. I can't go through what I went through before.

"I am going to tell you, but please don't interrupt until I'm done. Then if you need or want to ask questions, I will answer. You may decide to just leave," I murmur in a low voice.

I scoot off his lap and he looks so shattered that I take his hands in mine. I know I am fucking this up, although this is just as hard on me.

He looks me in the eyes as I begin, and I look downward. "When I was fifteen, I was kidnapped coming off a park trail. Debbie was with me when we were both taken. He ended up dumping her along the side of the roadway in a ditch. She laid there overnight until someone found her. He had beaten the bloody hell out of her and had left her for dead." I sniffle as I continue, "I was beaten bloody, broken bones, eyes were swollen shut, it took two months for the marks to heal on the outside. It's taken years for the emotional side to heal as much as it has. At first, I had a blindfold on, and he took it off. He always smelled like liquor and cigarettes. He reeked of them both. I was held for a week, although it felt like forever. I didn't know the difference in time. It felt like it was running all together. I thought there were two of them but only one ever came to the room I was held in. I remember crying for my daddy, 'Please help me daddy.' I wanted my momma. I cried so much I couldn't talk," I sob out in a tortured sound.

This is bringing up some very bad memories for me, and I am having flashbacks as I talk to Jax. "He raped me, over and over and over. Kept calling me vile names." Thinking to myself in my head. *'Bitch and cunt, whore, but I wasn't.'* I bawl intensely as I talk nonstop. "He beat me every single time he raped me. Every. Single. Time. He even started calling me by a name I didn't know.

My hands are shaking so badly Jax clasps them both in his hands to slow it down. He has tears running down his face.

He goes to say something, and I ask him to let me finish first. I have to get this out.

"He kept me on a nasty dirty smelly floor mat that smelled so bad I vomited more than once. I didn't even have a bucket to go to the bathroom in. My body was covered in urine and shit; that's one of the reasons I take so many showers to this day. He held me in a trailer, out of town. One day I heard a bunch of guns, people yelling. At first, I thought it was the television. Then I realized it wasn't. The door was slamming, and I could hear voices out in the other room. I just didn't know who it was. I was so frightened it would be someone else coming to hurt me. A lot of this time is still somewhat fuzzy to me, but I remember enough of it that I still have nightmares sometimes. I couldn't yell for help. I tried so hard. I had cried so much that I had hardly any sound left to make. I was in a locked room. Debbie's brothers found me. I wouldn't let anyone touch me. I was afraid of every little thing. Trent, one of Debbie's brothers, was the only one I would allow to touch me. I remember screaming at God in my mind and asking why he wouldn't help me. I kept screaming for my mom and dad. Pete is the one that killed him. I spent a week in the hospital. I couldn't let anyone in, I was still scared. Trent is my guardian angel. He took care of me for a long time after. I spent over two years in counseling. I didn't attend school for two years. I was homeschooled. A lot of it was kept quiet, but some of it still leaked out into the community. I was so ashamed at first. See I was no longer a virgin. He stole that from me." I hiccup and weep as I said all of this so fast, so I could get it out.

"I was finally rescued. I thought I was gonna die though. I didn't think I was ever going to get to go home," I bellow out in a howl, with tears running down my face like a faucet.

I feel Jax jerk. I look up and he looks so devastated. I have tears running down my face. He picks me up and puts me back in his lap, running his hands up and down my back.

He looks at me, lifts my chin so that I have to look him, "Who was he?" he growls. I jump a little and he looks contrite. "I'm sorry, please don't," he says to me in a whisper.

"A lot of what happened is still foggy. I don't know his name. They kept it from me," I tell him.

"Why would you think I would leave?" he says in a low voice.

"About three years ago, actually two and a half, I was dating a man. He was older than me, I thought I meant something to him. I told him what happened. Shortly thereafter, he started making comments that weren't so nice. See, I hadn't slept with him. He started calling me a prick tease, cunt, bitch, and other names. Then he hit me. Debbie's brother, Trent, had stopped by to see me and had seen him. He beat the hell out of him. I haven't seen him since. I told him I never wanted to see him again. On his way out the door, he told me I wanted what that other man did to me. That I lied about it." I weep so loud. I have snot running down my face. He hands me more Kleenex.

"I haven't dated or went with anyone since then. I know I freeze people out when they get too close. I don't want that with you, ever. You mean something to me. I mean you have seen some of my quirks. Making sure everything is locked, windows shut and locked, always looking around me to see if anyone is watching me. I don't go out after dark unless someone is with me. It would devastate me if you finally realized I was too much of a hassle to have a relationship with."

"Never," he growls. "You are mine. That means all of you. Remember what I said. I love you too, beautiful. We do this together. Is this why you shy away from making love with me?"

I nod. "Yeah, I haven't ever had sex with anyone... other than him," I state in such a sorrowful tone.

"Listen to me. You are a virgin in my eyes. He took. He stole from you. You didn't give that freely," he whispers with tears in his big expressive brown eyes. "You've had counseling?" He wants to know.

"Yes," I tell him. "I go to group meetings still to this day. I help others and also work a Rape Crisis Center line at least once a month. Honestly, I've been doing so well. Hardly any flashbacks or nightmares. The more I started to care for you, the worse the old came up. I knew I needed to talk to you. I was afraid. I don't want to lose you. Lately I have felt as if someone is watching me. I have had two nightmares and I hadn't had one in a long time. Doors being unlocked when I know I locked it and stuff like that."

"We will make sure everything is locked and bolted. Keep an eye out and see if we see someone following you," he replies.

He continues to touch me. He kisses the side of my head. He

taps the side of my leg. "I'm hungry, beautiful. Plus, I've missed you like crazy. Let's get up and go eat. You calm down some and I will ask my questions. Okay? Just know I am not leaving. I told you to always be honest and no cheating. I can't do either of those." He leans down and kisses me with such gentleness. I put my arms around his neck and hug him with such strength. My face must look a mess. My nose feels all swollen from crying and my eyes feel like they are gritty.

"I have really missed you too. I only made sloppy joes and fries. I'm sure the fries are cold by now. I can cook more," I tell him as I let go and walk into the kitchen.

I cook more fries in the air fryer this time and we eat. I take care of the kitchen for the night. He asks me where Sassy is, and I tell him she is still at Mom and Dad's.

He goes and grabs his things out of his car. He waves at Mrs. Franks and Pete who are standing across the street. I grin thinking about Pete's ass chewing. I told him. He didn't listen. Jax comes in, locks the door, checks to make sure everything is locked up tight, grabs my hand and drags me down the hall to the bedroom.

As soon as I cross the threshold, he shuts and locks that door too. He sets his bag on the bed. He tells me to hold on. He goes back out and comes in with a Diet Pepsi and a beer for himself. He re-locks the door. I smile. We sit on the loveseat in my bedroom sitting area. It's done in gray and teal colors. The loveseat is gray with teal printed toss pillows and blanket. I love to secretly sit here and read.

"Are you up to me asking questions?" Jax asks me in a low voice.

"Of course," I reply as I look him in the face, with a guarded expression on my face.

"Don't look at me like that, beautiful. This is me. How can I help if I don't know what you have been through?" he tells me in a determined but soft voice.

"Was Pete the police officer?"

"Yes, he was."

"You said you went to counseling?"

"Yes, I did, for two years solid. I wouldn't have made it otherwise. I became an emotional eater and gained about seventy-five pounds. It took a long time before I would even wear any clothing that showed skin. I thought If I was fat, guys wouldn't look at me. I was afraid to show my feminine side. I was afraid of my own shadow. I was afraid of the dark, and for a long time, afraid of everything. It's why I always lock everything up so tight. I used to shower with my underclothes on."

"You said Debbie was with you? Did they rape her as well?" I shake my head no.

"She has her own demons. She won't let me go to counseling with her. She still goes. That's how they knew I was taken. The police were doing everything they could to find us. It was Trent that actually found me. Him and his friends. Trent had Jimbo call Pete in," I tell him trying to put everything in the simplest way. This was bringing a lot of memories back. I'm rubbing my temples. I'm starting to get a headache. "I still have flashbacks with all of this. It's not you. Just, it's because I didn't know what to say. I wasn't really ready for the sexual part of our relationship until now. I think I'm ready. I mean..." As my voice trails off, my face blushes a nice rosy pink.

He leans down and kisses my nose. "Are you remembering that night?" he whispers.

I nod yes but won't look him in the face.

"Listen we are not making love tonight. It's been a long day and you look just wiped out. In all honesty, I am too. I've been so worried. I thought you were going to tell me to kick bricks, beautiful," he mutters to me in that deep sexy voice of his. "Let me go take a shower, sweets. I want to hold you in my arms. We will talk more later." As I tilt my head yes, he gets up and heads towards the bathroom. I am in bed waiting on him, trying to relax my muscles and thoughts. I see him come out of the bathroom... naked. I have just a night shirt on, but Jax is still naked.

"I thought we were gonna sleep, Jax," I say with a worried expression.

"We are but that doesn't mean I can't be comfortable, and you being in my arms, maybe on top of me for the night makes me comfortable," he retorts with an anxious grin on his face.

I climb up into his arms and get comfortable. He asks me if I am comfortable.

"Does a bear shit in the woods?" I utter.

He laughs out loud. "I miss your smartass."

"I'm glad, cause I kind of like her too. She is a friend of mine and keeps me on an even-keel," I tell him in all honesty.

I tell him some of my hopes and dreams. I tell him a little more of what happened the week I was held. I tell him I want to be one hundred percent healed. I tell him I want a life with him.

CHAPTER ELEVEN

He holds me all night long. He knew that I wasn't ready and didn't push. I wake up slowly to him rubbing his hands up and down my back. No pressure, just soothingly. "You are so beautiful," he tells me. He keeps looking with his eyes roving all over my face. He bends down, and so softly kisses me again. He presses his face into the crook of my neck and keeps kissing me all over. He rolls over and grabs my hands. "Let's go take a quick shower."

We get out of the shower and get dressed. I am trying to show more on the physical side of things, more hugging and kissing, holding hands but I still am not really ready. I know that, Jax understands. We have talked about this and he promised he wouldn't give up on us, me. We will work this out, he says this to me this all the time.

He leans down, kisses my nose. "Do you remember when you put my cock in your mouth and played with it like a lollipop? Remember when I gave you my cum and you took it down your throat? That was the hottest thing I have ever seen. I am waiting for that to happen again, but what I'm really looking forward to is the first time I get to come in your pussy. Do you know how much action my fist has gotten? My fist should be sprained, I've jacked off so much," he whispers in my ear, just low enough that I have shivers racing all over my body. My nipples are as hard as little pebbles.

"I don't know if I am ready, Jax. I want to, but I'm scared. What twenty-five-year-old is afraid to have sex," I mutter.

"Sweetheart, we'll know when you're ready. I can wait, this is on your time schedule." He is holding the side of my face as he tells me this. He leans in and kisses me on my lips.

"Now, let's go for a ride or something today." With a smile I agree. I know he is the one for me.

CHAPTER TWELVE

ONE MONTH LATER

This past month everything has been going great. I didn't know it but Jax's place is above the tattoo shop. It has two apartments and Toby lives in the other one. Sassy and I stay there a lot. She even has her own bed, food bowls, toys and bath stuff. Jax loves that baby as much as me. Tonight, I am on my way there with Sassy and groceries. Before I left my house, I felt as if someone was watching me again, although I never did see anyone or anything out of place. I made sure to lock up tight because we're staying here at Jax's for the weekend. It's been quiet around my place. Mrs. Franks isn't talking to me and Pete hasn't been around much. I guess I need to make her some cookies as an apology.

Trent called to see how I was doing. We talked and got caught up on things for about an hour. It seemed like he asked a lot of questions about Debbie and Toby. Yes, they are now seeing each other.

As I am driving, I think back to the night that Jax and I made love. I had woken up and was curled up in his arms. I was running my hands up and down his body. His cock stood up to the attention it was receiving. My God was it standing up. I was the one to instigate our love-making for the first time. I was so ready this time, and he was so fucking gentle with me. He talked to me the whole time, whispering words of encouragement, leading me through it all. It was perfect. It was more than I ever imagined it could be. As the time has gone on, he has become more demanding as a lover. I love it. It's no longer all kid gloves. He loves me like a man should love his woman. I am brought out of my reminiscing as I see the shop up ahead.

After I park in the rear of the shop, I grab as much as I can and head inside to the back of the shop. Zeke, one of Jax employees just pulled up and hollers, asking if there is anything he can grab. I tell him my bag and another bag of groceries. He tells me he'll take them upstairs for me, and I thank him. He's kind of quiet, but he has a lot on his plate with raising his younger sister. He's single, so he doesn't get a lot of help. He and sister lost their parents in an automobile accident. He's only twenty-eight, his sister is nine years old. He got custody of her when she was six, but from what I hear his parents identified him as his sister guardian in the will. It's been an adjustment for the both of them from what Jax has told me. Jax makes sure that Zeke gets home in time to take care of her, after school. On the weekends, she spends some time at the shop with him. He seems to be a nice guy, with a lot of responsibility, but he does a great job.

I set everything on the steps and drop Sassy to the floor. Off she goes causing all kinds of havoc in the parlor. I can hear Samantha talking to her as well as Toby. I hear the machines going to town, so, I know the guys have customers. My man hollers out that he's almost done, and Sassy makes a beeline for his room. "Yap, yap, yap," is all I hear. Jax laughs and I hear a female laugh too. I freeze on the spot; the green-eyed jealousy bug just hit. Sounds stupid. I know he tats other females, but I've never been around when he has.

I take a deep breath and holler for Sassy. She refuses to come out. I tap on the door and Jax tells me to come on in. The lady is holding Sassy as Jax is finishing up a tattoo on her foot. She's pretty, but I can tell I've nothing to worry about. He looks at me and smirks. He's getting pretty good at reading my mind nowadays. He introduces us. She is a friend of Cassie's. Wow, now I really feel like a fool. We exchange pleasantries, as he cleans and wraps the tattoo up. He is done with this client, and ready for his last one of the day. She hands me Sassy on her way out the door to go pay. Jax pats my ass as he follows her.

Muttering under my breath to Sassy I call her a traitor. She smiles that doggy smile at me. Jax comes back in as I'm cleaning up the chair and counters for him. I throw the used needles away. I also start up a new tray with items on a clean surface after washing my hands. He looks at me, grabs me around my waist, puts his hand up under my shirt, and unhooks my bra. "Jax, honey, you have another client coming in." I moan as I tell him this. God, this man, he makes me so fucking horny. I never knew it could be like this. I am so totally head over heels in love with him.

I hear someone clear their throat as Jax has his tongue shoved in my mouth. I am trying to catch my breath, as I tap him on his shoulder.

"Jax, your client is here." He isn't stopping. I tap harder but on his side. He starts to sit in his chair with me on top of him.

More throat clearing.

"*Jax.*" His name is long and drawn out with humor "Dammit, Jax, this isn't the time." Toby laughs out loud with a yell.

"Toby, if you don't get the hell out of here, I am going to whip your ass," Jax growls in a pissed-off tone.

By this time, I am up and bent over laughing like an outrageous crazy person.

"What the hell are you laughing at, beautiful?" he growls at me.

"This is like being at my house," I tell him with an amused pig snort laugh.

He gets up and pushes Toby out the door. He backs me up against it and kisses me again. "This will commence later tonight, upstairs," he tells me.

Smiling at him, I tell him, "Okay, handsome, until later."

He leans in and kisses me again. He loves to give me hot wet juicy kisses everywhere, and I mean *everywhere*.

"I have to take my stuff upstairs. I'm going to unpack the groceries and make dinner. That's after I take a shower," I let him know.

"Hold on and I will help get it upstairs. Samantha can you lead Matt back, I need to take some stuff upstairs. Let him know I will be right back."

"Sure Jax," Samantha replies.

We head up with everything I brought over. I go and start putting things away.

"Beautiful, let's just order in tonight. You look tired and I just want to sit and spend time with you. You're are always cleaning here and at your place."

"Sure, if you want too," I tell him in a low deep mysterious sexy voice, eyes half hooded with a come-hither look.

"You're getting really good with them looks, beautiful."

"Thank you. I've been working on them."

He shakes his head giving me a smooch on the lips on his way out the door. Sassy is barking. I tell her to be good, as I go and start my shower. I am getting *lucky,* tonight. I lay down on the bed after my shower, wrapped in a towel. I am so tired tonight. I really need to go in for a check-up. I haven't been feeling all that well the last week. I really think I'm coming down with a cold. I've had the sniffles the last couple of days. Lying on the bed, I look at the clock, and it's only five-thirty. I close my eyes for just a minute and that's the last thing I remember.

"Hey, beautiful," I hear as I feel the bed move a little.

I move a little and smile while my eyes are still closed. "Hey, handsome, what time is it? I must have dozed off for a minute."

"It's seven in the evening, beautiful. You okay?" he inquires with worry in his voice.

"I'm okay. I haven't been feeling up to par. I think I'm starting to come down with a cold or something," I tell him.

He looks at me and feels my forehead. "You don't feel warm," he whispers. "Are you hungry, beautiful?"

"A little, honey," I tell him with a small impish look.

We decide to just make chicken noodle soup and sandwiches for supper. I get ready to take Sassy outside but Jax has already taken her out. I reach over and give him a gigantic hug. I feel loved by him. *He takes my breath away,* I'm thinking to myself.

"You take my breath away too," he states with a smile so bright it lights up his face, and mine too.

"I spoke out again, didn't I?"

"Yep, I love it too, because I know what you're thinking a lot of the time and it's nice to know these things."

We eat dinner after I warm us up some soup. We sit and watch a movie on tv with Jax getting handsy by the minute.

"I love you, handsome," I repeat again with a sparkle in my gaze.

"I love you to Ria. You've become my world. It gets easier doesn't it, honey?" he says with a big blooming grin on his face.

"Yes, it has. You have made it easier," I reply. We cuddle for the rest of the show and head back to bed. Jax takes Sassy outside again for me. It's been awhile, but I still remember the night we made love for the first time. I was so turned on. I think I would have hurt him if he had stopped. He was patient and so loving towards me. He went so slow, talked to me. I had seven orgasms that night. I couldn't walk for a day or two. I was a little sore too.

We are crawling into bed when he comes up behind me. "Back up, honey, and tilt them beautiful hips for me. I need this pussy now." he growls out.

I do as he says, and he runs his fingers in and around my pussy. I'm already so wet; it really doesn't take much when it comes to him. God, I love it. He starts to finger fuck me from behind. He is using his other hand to jerk off a little. He leans forward, removes his finger and runs his dick up and down my slit. He gets his cock all wet with my juices, lines it up and slams inside of me, grabbing my hips at the same time. He continues to slam inside me short jabbing strokes, then long strokes. He doesn't slow down at all.

"Are you almost there, beautiful?" he asks.

I snarl, "I want more. More," I repeat. "Don't stop," I whimper out. "Jax, I am so close. Don't you dare stop," I demand of him. He reaches around and pushes his finger on my clit with pressure. I detonate. I come and come some more. My pussy is rippling around his dick. He keeps pounding into me and roars so loud, that there is banging on the wall.

He collapses on top of me, kissing the side of my head. "It gets better every time, beautiful. *Every time*," he whispers.

We clean up and crawl into bed. I want to go back home, and I want him to move in with me. I need my home. I will mention it in the morning.

CHAPTER THIRTEEN

"Jax, we need to consider staying at my place for a while." I stop getting dressed so I can hopefully catch his full attention this morning. "It would be so much easier on me to leave from work in the mornings at my place with Sassy there. She is running amuck at your place of business downstairs and one of these days someone may report you, I don't want that to happen. Most of all, I kind of miss my place. I worked so hard to make it a home for me." I look him in the face as I tell him this to see what kind of reaction I will get.

"Are you asking me to move in with you, beautiful?" he asks with a soft expression. He leans forward and nabs me around the waist, as I lean forward for my pants, so I can continue getting dressed for work. I drop my pants as he does this, and they fall to the floor.

I gaze up into his eyes, a look of pure happiness on my face when he understands immediately what I'm asking. I'm nodding my head yes so fast I could get whiplash.

"Yes, I am. I don't think I could sleep without you now," I eagerly say with a blinding smile.

"I will start moving some stuff in today. Do you have an extra key, baby?" he asks me.

"I do. Do you want to stop by and pick it up at the shop or wait until tonight?" I ask him.

"I'll stop by and take you out for lunch before I move some stuff in. Where do you want me to put my things?"

"Just move my clothes over in the closet to one side. I have enough room for your things too." I am so happy I'm glowing.

"We will have to get a dresser for you. There is enough room in the bedroom for it though. Some of your extra stuff can go in the spare bedroom or that closet in there. Is that okay?"

"I have some tools and stuff I need to bring. Do you have enough room in the garage for my motorcycle and toolbox?" he eagerly wants to know.

"More than enough. My car is outside until winter sets in and I know it's going to snow. I hate to clean off the windows, so maybe you'll do that now?" I impishly say to him.

"Anything for you, beautiful. *Anything,*" he says with truthfulness.

I reach up and grab his beard, bringing him a little lower so I can lean in and grab his lips with mine. I kiss and then nip at his lips until he opens up and I tangle my tongue with his. I moan deep and low in my throat. I love this man. *He owns my soul. Owns It.*

He puts his hands on my ass and lifts me up and down we go on the bed. He fits himself in between my legs.

He is reaching around taking off his and my clothing as fast as he can.

"This is going to be fast, beautiful. I have a client due in twenty minutes. So, I mean it's gonna be fast."

I moan as he takes his finger and runs it through the lips of my pussy. It's so wet, it slides right through and into my cunt. He starts finger fucking me as his tongue mimics fucking my mouth. He always turns me on so fast. My hands run up and down his body fast and feverishly as I want them too. I reach down in between us and I grab his big thick long cock in my hand. He is leaking pre-cum all over my leg as I smear it up and down his shaft.

"Enough, Ria. I'm coming in that gorgeous pussy of yours this time. Let go, baby." He huskily murmurs.

He grabs my hand, pinning it above my head. I go to freeze a little and with a shake of his head, he groans, "Trust me, baby." He lets go and I leave my hand where he had placed it above my head. He takes his cock and rubs it up and down the lips of my pussy. He gets it coated with my juices from my cunt and slowly enters me with determination. We rock against each other and continue on that way. I can feel my climax building. He looks down, rears up on his knees, grabs my hips and slams home faster and more forcefully than ever before.

"Ria, honey, you need to catch up. I'm about to come." He groans feverishly.

"I'm almost there," I moan.

"Take your fingers and get yourself there faster. Hurry, Ria," he growls.

I do as he says, and not twenty seconds later I am screaming through my orgasm.

Jax grunts long and loud, "I love you, beautiful," as he comes inside of me.

He is laying on top of me, when his phone starts ringing. He picks it up.

"Hello, Toby, what do you need?" he says.

"Shit, yes, please get him a cup of coffee for me and I will be right down."

He hangs his phone up.

"Honey, I gotta get dressed and you are late too. Leave Sassy and I will take her home with me when I come get my key," he says with a sigh. "They are always interrupting us," he says complaining.

"We have two businesses to run, honey. It's our life." I smack his ass and tell him to move it.

I jump up, run to the bathroom and clean up a little. *Good thing I'm on birth control,* I think as I finish getting dressed again. I pet Sassy on my way to the door, grabbing up my folder and purse on my way out. I am going to be late getting there. My first client is usually five minutes late every time though, so I should be good.

I holler out that I am leaving as I exit the back door.

"Have a good day beautiful," Jax says with his voice raised so I can hear him.

"You too, handsome," I tell him.

The drive to the salon doesn't take long. The sun is so bright this morning, but it is a little cooler. Soon it's going to be fall and the leaves will change color and fall from their branches. Winter has always reminded me of death for some reason. I love the holidays but not the weather. I love the spring the most, it reminds me of rebirth.

I pull into the side parking lot, but when I get out I have chills up and down my neck and arms. I hurriedly look around and take my keys and point one through two fingers with my thumb holding it in place. I know someone is watching, but I don't see who it is. This seems to be happening more. I need to tell Pete about this. I hurry into the salon and all the ladies are there today. I have a ton of clients coming in today; I hope that I don't get too far behind.

I tell all the girls good morning. I go to the office and drop off my things as I grab my overcoat that I wear for working. It saves me a lot of money because it protects my clothing. I get out front and call back my first client for the day. We have all been so busy none of us realize the time until Jax walks through the door with Toby. I raise my eyebrow and look at Toby.

Jax laughs. "He wants to help me move today. He doesn't have any more clients until later this evening."

Toby turns and glares at Jax. "Yeah, I'm helping you move so I can get some damn sleep. You guys going at it all the damn time, I can't get any fucking sleep," he complains.

Jax reaches around and slaps the piss out of him. "Watch your mouth Toby, we are not at the shop where they're used to that type of language. You're around ladies now," he spits out in reprimand.

"Sorry ladies," Toby tells everyone in the salon. Of course, with that smile all is forgiven.

"Give me ten minutes and I'll be done, handsome," I let him know.

He nods his head okay. They both head back to my office to wait on me. I turn around and finish styling my clients hair.

The ladies are all done about the same time, so Alexis goes and locks the front door for lunch and hangs the sign that says we will return at one-thirty.

I look out the window and see traffic picking up some. I turn and head towards the back to the office. I hear the guys talking.

"Are you sure this is what you want to do, Jax? This is a big step," Toby asks with a voice that sounds opposed to us being together.

"Yes, Toby, I'm sure. I love that woman. You have no idea of what she has been through. You need to come to terms with whatever feelings you have against her. I am not having this conversation again," he says with a growl that shows he is getting pissed off.

"Look, Jax, I don't know what happened to her because you won't tell me. What I do know is whatever it is, she has made Debbie feel like it's her fault. She is always worried more about Ria than herself. It's wrong. Whatever happened, she shouldn't make Debbie feel like it's her fault. She is supposed to be her best friend, and friends don't treat friends that way," he mutters.

"Get the hell out of here, Toby, before I kick your ass. You have no idea what you're talking about. You better never say anything like this in front of Ria. I mean it, Toby. Until you can be nice and mind your own business, stay away," he spits out furiously.

I have tears running down my face. I have no idea of what is going on. *Does Debbie really feel this way?* We have always been honest with one another, is it true what Toby's saying? I hear Toby coming towards me, so I turn to leave, and he sees me. He sees my tears, gives me a pissed-off look and leaves without saying a word.

Jax is on the phone now, with whom I have no idea. I don't want to know at this point as I turn and go to the bathroom to mop up my face and get it together.

I need to talk to Debbie and find out what's going on. Jax comes and asks if I'm ready. I tell him that I forgot I had a late client coming in and where I kept my spare key. He said he was gonna go ahead then and he would see me later tonight.

"Okay, Jax. I'll see you then," I mumble through the doorway.

"You okay, beautiful?" he hesitantly asks.

"Fine, honey. I'll see you tonight," I repeat.

I hear him leave and stay in the bathroom for an extra few minutes to make sure he's gone.

I go into my office, close and lock the door. I get my purse and take out my phone. I look to see if Debbie ever called me back from yesterday. She hasn't, so I call her number, but it goes straight to voicemail. I call her mom and ask Jackie if she's seen her.

"Ria, honey, how are you?" she wants to know.

"Doing good," I reply. "Have you talked to Debbie?" I ask.

"Yesterday, before she left to go to Tennessee to see Trent. She didn't tell you?" she asks.

"No, she hasn't returned any of my calls. At first, I didn't think anything of it and now I'm worried. Momma Jackie, a friend of hers says that it's my fault she isn't getting any better and that I blame her for what happened to me. I'm worried now. I don't know what to do," I say as I sob out loud.

"Oh, honey, we know it's not your fault and she knows it too. She stopped going to counseling a while back. Said she didn't need it anymore. She needs to go back. I hope that Trent can reach her while she's down there," she whispers to me.

"I'm so sorry, I haven't been there for her lately. If you talk to her, would you tell her I miss and love her and to call me, please?" I ask

"I will, honey. Don't you worry about this, Ria. It's her fault for stopping the therapy. We can't make her go," she answers.

"Okay, Momma Jackie. I love you guys." I gasp out with heartache.

We say goodbye and hang up. I call Trent, he picks up on the first ring.

"She's gonna be okay, sweets. I promise. She's back in counseling. Who the hell is this new guy she's seeing?" he demands.

"It's Jax's brother, Toby," I tell him.

"He needs to stop pushing her so much. It's not helping her any at all. He doesn't want me to pay him a visit," Trent states harshly. I sniffle out loud. "What's happened, sweets?" he asks me. I let him know it's nothing.

"Things are changing. Jax is moving in and I miss my best friend. Will you tell her I love and miss her, please?" I ask him.

"Congratulations on moving forward, honey. I love you, kiddo. I'm always here for you. You remember that," he says with happiness in his voice. "She knows you love her. I'll make sure she knows to call soon. Okay?"

"I love you, Trent. Thank you for everything." We hang up from one another and I sit down and email Debbie a long email. I know she'll read it.

Hey Debbie,
Damn there is a lot going on, and I feel like I am adrift with not sharing it with you. I wish I knew what I could do to help you. I miss you so fucking much. There are days that I feel my life is out of control, and you aren't here to listen to me rant like a smartass. You know how some take offense to smartassness. You understand that part of me, and you laugh with me. Jax is moving in. Toby is being an asshole, and I don't have the first clue what I've done to him. I love his brother. He just seems so

moody, out of touch with reality sometimes. I keep asking your mom and dad about you. I talked to Trent today to see if you were busy. I know you have a lot going on, so I decided to send you an email. I asked again if I could come see you, but he told me you weren't ready. I love you. Please reach out. This is a two-way street, you have always been my rock, let me be yours. You have always been here for me. Let me be there for you. Tell me what I can do to help you. If it's something I've done, tell me so I can fix it. I miss you, please know I am here. I love you too the moon and back, Sis. You call me anytime night or day. I am here for you. Your sister from another set of parents,

Ria......

xoxoxoxoxoxo

I work the rest of the afternoon at the salon. I have done a total of twenty heads of hair today; I am tired and worn out. I just want to go home, take a shower, eat and go to bed. We all finish cleaning the salon and we all head out at the same time. I get in my car and head home. I have missed it there. I like to surround myself with familiar things. I feel better and safer. I am still so upset about Toby. He needs to stop with this crap. This is the second time he's butting in where he shouldn't. The first time I excused him because it was his brother. This is going too far.

I get home and there are Jax and his parents. He looks like he got his things moved in. There's a trailer that is sitting in the driveway that looks empty except for a dresser.

I park and get out, put a smile on my face even if it looks fake. I am so glad he's here, but I'm nervous about Toby causing us problems. He has been pretty vocal about his dislike of me lately; actually, it's been from the start. His parents come out of the house, his mom holding Sassy in her arms. Jax sees me, stops the direction he is heading, and makes a beeline to me. He stops when he gets there, picking me up, and carries me through the threshold of the house. He kisses me as he sets me down, keeping his hands on my ass.

"I have almost everything moved in," he says in a deep bass sounding happy voice.

"Any problems with anything?" I ask as I slide my hands up and around his neck. I lean in and nip at his lips. I love his beard, it's so soft on my face. He takes over the kiss like always, deepening it with a sweep of his tongue to the outside of my lips demanding entrance and he will not be denied.

His dad comes inside with drawers to the dresser, and I tap his shoulders to get his attention. He leans back, and his lips are glistening from our kiss.

"It just got a lot better," he responds with a cocky tooth-showing grin.

I shake my head not believing a word of it.

"Hi, Stewart and Eva, how are you all doing today? Did he keep you all busy?" I ask.

His dad grunts.

Eva tells me they had a great day; it's not often they get to spend time together like this.

"Sassy kept you entertained?"

"I love this little baby. She is a sweetheart," she replies.

Jax leans down and kisses me and goes out the door to get the dresser. I glance out and he lifts the rest of it by himself and starts his way in. I see Mrs. Franks outside waving like a loon. Then I see Jax's face turn bright cherry red, it continues down his neck and he drops the dresser on the ground.

I head outside and so does Eva.

"Well, sonny, are you gonna come work on my plumbing or not? It's just a little rust, what's it gonna hurt? Big strong lad like you, wouldn't take long at all," she gleefully declares with a flamboyant twist of her hips.

I just hang my head as Jackie sounds like she is choking on her tongue. I twist my head in her direction and tell her I am so sorry. She looks at me and cracks up laughing harder than I have ever seen anyone laugh.

Jax turns and looks at me.

"Your decision, honey bun," I tell him with a wicked look on my face. His mom laughs even harder. Mrs. Franks has totally gotten out of hand. I have decided to sit this one out and let him figure it out on his own. He is going to have to one up her for her to stop. I smother a grin with my hand. I look at him with a twinkle in my eyes.

Jax looks at Mrs. Franks and tells her again that he is a one-woman man. She has a devious look on her face now, and I know she is up to no good. He hasn't figured it out yet. He will.

Eva and Stewart stay for dinner that Eva had cooked while I was at work. They are great people and I am happy to have them in my life.

"Why didn't Toby come help today Jax?" his dad asks with a smile.

Jax looks at his parents with a pissed-off look.

"Toby is being an ass, stepping over boundaries and not being really nice to Ria or myself. I have no idea what his problem is, but he had my woman crying today. I won't have it. I will whip his ass if he does it again." he states with a voice filled with deep gritty pissed-off male testosterone.

"How did you know that?" I ask with an expression full of disbelief.

"I know you. I heard you trying to cover it up. If he hadn't of already left, I would have beat him today. Beautiful, you come first for me. He will not disrespect you again. He has no business butting in when he doesn't know nothing. Apparently, Debbie hasn't told him," he states empathetically.

"She stopped going to counseling, she's now visiting Trent. I talked with him today. She is back in therapy, but not taking my calls. She has always blamed herself. She won't accept that she saved me." I say with tears running down my face.

I just now realize that I have talked about what happened to Debbie and I with his parents in the house and I am mortified. I look over and excuse myself and leave the room. I sob with hiccups. I go to the bathroom to mop myself up. I am gone for about five minutes when I go back to the table. They all look up. I can tell Jax has been talking to them just from the look in their eyes.

"I didn't tell them everything, beautiful. That's for when you are ready."

I just nod. I sit down and decide they need to know some of what happened. "When I was fifteen, I was kidnapped and held for a week. Debbie was with me; they took her and beat her really badly and dumped her in a ditch. She laid there for well over fifteen hours. I was raped and was hurt pretty badly myself. I had intensive counseling for a long time." I tell them all of this with tears running down my face. Jax is up and squatting down next to me on the floor. He has wrapped his hand around my neck kissing the side of my head.

"Honestly, I prefer for this to not go any further. It was all pretty much kept hush hush. Debbie's brother, Trent, found me and her other brother, Pete, helped to keep it buried. Pete's a police officer. I don't have any idea why Debbie blames herself. Counseling helps, but she also won't let me go with her, or anyone else. I have a hard time letting others that are not victims know my story," I whisper. I am still looking down and not seeing their reaction.

When I look up finally, they both have tears running down their faces. His mom is weeping quietly. I look at Jax. "I am so proud of you, beautiful. Thank you for sharing with them," he tells me gently under his breath.

It takes a few minutes for everyone to get themselves together.

"Since Toby and Debbie are seeing each other, I can't and won't say anything of what went down. She hasn't told him, otherwise he wouldn't be acting this way, I don't think. If he does know then I am sorry, because he's just a dick then. If he doesn't, then it's not my place to tell him," I say with a forceful strong voice.

His parents agree to not say a word to anyone.

"It's none of his business, that little asshole. I am going to kick his ass too if he doesn't stop," Stewart says.

"I'm going to smack that child upside his head," Eva mutters at the same time.

It's late and has been a long day. Honestly, I am just ready to go to sleep. I have cried more in the last month than I have in the last year. His parents give us both hugs and kisses.

Jax shuts and locks the front door. I smile. He is learning some of my quirks and that makes me love him that much more. I clean things up, and Jax lets Sassy outside. I am wiping off the counters when he comes back in from the back of the house, he turns to the back door and lets Sassy back inside.

"Let's take a shower, beautiful. I am worn out and I know you are too."

He takes my hand and we turn off the lights as we head down the hallway. He shuts the bedroom door and we head toward the bathroom. I stop and look around. I can see Jax's belongings mixed in with mine. I look at him with love in my eyes. "I'm so glad you're moved in with me. I love you, Jax."

He takes me in his arms, with his mouth by my ear and softly says, "I love you too, beautiful, more than I thought imaginable."

We get in the shower and wash each other. We get out with drops of water running down our bodies. He takes a towel and dries me off, then himself as I brush my teeth. He comes over and grabs his own toothbrush and brushes his. He's looking at me in the mirror as we get ready for bed side by side. I rinse my toothbrush and head toward the bed. I pull the covers back as he picks me up from behind. He places me in the middle of the bed, scoots in behind me, and wraps his arms around me. He kisses me. "Sleep baby. We have the rest of our lives. I have to do one tattoo in the morning then I'll be home. Shouldn't take more than a couple of hours. Stay in bed and rest. If you aren't feeling any better, you need to go to the walk-in clinic," he tells me.

"Honey you worry too much. I am just overly stressed, being worried about your reaction, and everything else in our life. I will be back to my old self as soon as I get some rest."

"You heard what I said. If you are not any better you are going."

I drift off to sleep for the first time in my home with my man living here. I feel loved and cherished.

CHAPTER FOURTEEN

Things are going well; we have been living together for about six weeks. Jax and Toby have a strained relationship right now, and I feel a little like I am stuck in the middle. This is his brother, there shouldn't be that line drawn between them. Toby is blaming me for Debbie being gone, and she isn't taking any of his calls. He also doesn't understand how she can financially not work either, but that's her story to tell. His family have been over for a cookout, but Toby made excuses not to come. In all honesty, it was probably for the best. My parents adore Jax, and Sophia can't wait to meet him.

It's Friday, and it's getting cooler with fall setting in. It's about two weeks before Halloween.

"Jax, honey, I think I want to go see Debbie. We haven't ever gone this long without seeing each other and I miss her something awful. I'm also worried about her." I look at him as I am saying this.

He glances over. "If you want to go, then go. If you want me to take you, I will take you. It's up to you," he says with a look of understanding.

"I'll call today at lunch and check in first to see how she's doing. I will also ask Trent before I decide for sure. I only have a small load today, so I will be getting off a little early. How does your day look?" I ask looking at him.

"I have a full load today. Not sure what time I will get off but will try to get home as early as I can. I took tomorrow off. Just a day at home for a change, but I also have a surprise for you too. I want to get the yard cleaned up one last time and change the oil on my bike."

"Okay, I love you, honey." I reach up and rake my fingers through his beard and tug his head down, this is one of the many ways of how I get my kisses from him. He always grins at me, because I rub my hands through his beard. He smacks my ass on my way out the door. "Let Sassy out please, before you leave. He nods his head. He's doing something on his phone. Heck, he could be ordering supplies for all I know.

It's been a long day at the salon, and I tried to get ahold of both Debbie and Trent. No answer from either of them so I have no idea of what's going on. I head home and as I get out, I felt as if someone had been watching me as I pulled into my driveway. It's starting to irritate the piss out of me. I holler at Mrs. Franks and she asks for her cookies. I tell her next week, maybe. I unlock the front door and go inside and lock the door behind me. I go to let Sassy out. She is running around my feet, crazy like. The back door wasn't locked. I look around but don't see anything out of place. I grab a knife and head down the hallway. I look around and nothing looks out of place there either. I just think maybe Jax forgot to lock the door. I will have to remind him to do that. I hear someone knocking and go and look out. Trent is on the porch looking around. I see he is waving at Mrs. Franks. She always did like him. I open the door and squeal like a teenager. I love this big lug. He wraps his arms around me, leans in and give me a big kiss. I laugh and let him in.

"So, I tried calling earlier. I didn't know you were coming up." I say with a smile.

"I know, sweets. I brought Debbie home to Mom and Dad's. She's doing better, and I expect she will be by to see you in the next few days. She went into inpatient therapy this time. She looks good, seems to be doing so much better. I told her what your man's brother was doing. She wants nothing to do with him now," he says. We sit and visit for about an hour. I tell him I am one hundred percent in love with Jax. He is really happy for me. He wants to get back to the clubhouse before the party tonight he says with a big lecherous smile on his face. I just shake my head, grin and stick my tongue out at him. Childish I know but it reminds me of my childhood.

"Hey before you leave, I want to mention that sometimes I feel like someone is watching me. I look around but don't see anyone *but...*" I trail off.

He looks a little concerned and tells me he will look into it.

"Have you said anything to Pete?" he wants to know. I shake my head no.

He hugs me again and he leaves. It's now six-thirty and Jax should be home in the next hour. I go back in and start dinner. I'm making spaghetti; it's one of Jax's favorites.

It's going on seven-thirty and he isn't home yet. I go get my phone because I heard it go off earlier. It's a message from some unknown number. It's a picture of Trent kissing me on my porch. *What the hell?* I think to myself. *Why would someone be taking a picture of Trent kissing me?*

I try calling Jax and there is no answer. I wait for another hour and he still isn't home. I continue to try to call him and the shop. I finally call and ask Eva if she's heard from him. She tells me she had seen him earlier and he said he had plans to go out with a friend for a drink and he had something else to do. He stopped by and grabbed some clothes; she told me that the kids have always left spares at the house. I asked her if she hears from him if she would have him call me. She said she would.

I wait up all night, worried sick. He never called home. I'm silently crying, not understanding what in the hell is going on. I continue to look at my phone to see if he has messaged me. I've laid on this damn couch waiting for him to come home all night. My phone dings again. I look and it's another picture. He has a girl in his arms, in a bed. I set my phone down and just bawl like a baby. He was so adamant that he wouldn't tolerate cheating, and there he is doing it himself. That son of a bitch.

I take a shower and start cleaning my home. Although I have been up all night, I have things to take care of, like packing up his shit in trash bags. I will not be treated this way. I work all day gathering his things and am exhausted and end up falling asleep around ten that night.

I wake up the next day at seven in the morning with my face ravaged. I decide to put a cold compress on my face to help with the effects of crying. The doorbell rings at nine and it's Toby. I open the door and let him in. I look like hell and he just has this look of pure glee on his face.

"What do you want Toby?" I ask, not in the mood for his bullshit.

"Jax wanted me to come get some of his clothes. He said to tell you he doesn't like cheaters, do not call him, do not come to the shop. *He said it was over.* He also said he would be by in the next week to get the rest of his things," he tells me with mirth in his voice.

"Sure, Toby, here are his clothes. Tell him to let me know when, and I will make myself scarce. He can leave the key on the table," I mutter.

He grabs up the bags of clothes and out the door he goes. After I see him off, it pops in my head that he wasn't surprised that Jax's clothes were already packed up. Almost as if he knew they would be. I wonder if he is the one that I feel watching me.

I lock it all up and go crawl back into bed. I still am not feeling well and I do need to go to the doctor tomorrow. I drift off to sleep crying silently. I wake up later to a headache so bad I'm vomiting. My ears hurt, and I have a temperature. I get dressed in sweats and go take myself to the urgent care in town. I'm in and out in just under an hour. I have an upper respiratory infection and they put me on steroids and antibiotics. They told me if I don't start feeling better in the next three days to come back. I go to the pharmacy and get the prescriptions filled before heading home. I pull up and there sits Jax. *What the hell?* He already sent his lap dog over, did he come to see what he has reduced me too. As far as I'm concerned, love isn't what it's all cracked up to be. It's nothing but a lot of heartache. I get out of my vehicle and give him an evil eye. "What do you want Jax?" I ask with a tired voice.

"Why?" he asks.

"Why what?"

"Why did you send my clothes back to me? Why didn't you talk to me before doing that?" he asks me.

My mouth falls open.

"Look I don't know what you're going on about. *You* sent your brother over for your clothes. You're the one with another girl in bed, and you're the one who hasn't returned any of my calls after my calling countless times. You went out with a friend; I didn't know anything about it, not even a common courtesy of you letting me know you were going. So, don't throw this shit at me. You promised no cheating, you were adamant that *you* wouldn't tolerate it, and look what you did the first chance you got." I keep getting louder with each word uttered. I am so mad at him. I am so sick that he done this to us.

"I wasn't the one to cheat. You were. Toby said he had seen you," he mutters and goes to grab me.

I drop my purse and lunge towards him and drop kick his knee. He goes down. I am standing there wheezing and out of breath, partly because I am so pissed off, the other because I am sicker than a dog. Just as I am about to pick up my things off the ground, Pete pulls up and gets out of his vehicle. He looks around and takes in the scene. He raises his eyebrow, concern on his face.

"What the hell is going on?" he forcefully asks, as he looks at Jax on the ground.

I look at Pete. "I want him gone," pointing my finger at Jax.

I pick up my purse and go toward the door. Turning back around, yelling at Pete, "Get my fucking house key while you're taking out the trash."

I go in and lock the door behind me. I can hear the two arguing and just keep heading toward the kitchen. I get my medicine out along with something for my temperature and take them all with a glass of milk. I let Sassy out and wait on her. I hear someone knock. I stalk toward the front door and yank it open.

I answer the door, with my hand held out, waiting for Pete to put my key in my hand. I snatch it up and before he can ask, I slam the door in his face.

I let Sassy back in and go to bed, turning the television on just for the noise and company. Tears are running down my face, but they are pissed-off tears. *How dare he.* He's the one that cheated. I didn't. I'm so damn angry, so fucking heartbroken.

I drift off to sleep, praying the nightmares don't start in the middle of the night. I wake up to gut-wrenching tears streaming down my face. My pillow is soaked from my tears. I grab it up and hold it wishing it was Jax. *Why did he have to fuck it all up?* I am rocking myself back and forth in my bed. Sassy gets up in my lap trying to nudge her way up into my arms, I pick her up and hold her. Jax kept the nightmares from appearing and now they're back with a vengeance. I get up, head into the kitchen to get something to drink, and sit on the couch. Sassy gets up and wants in my arms again. She knows something is wrong. I pet her and tell her what my nightmare was, just like I used too. She can't talk me out of it though. As the tears continue to fall, she tries to lick them all away.

I sit until daybreak light sifts through the curtains by the front window. I get up to make a cup of coffee, and it feels so good on my throat, the warmth of it. Now, I wish the ice I feel in my veins would thaw. My phone is ringing, and I answer it without looking at who it is.

"Talk to me, Ria. Did you have another nightmare?" Jax asks me. I look at the phone wondering how the hell he knew. I put the phone back to my ear. "I'm sitting outside. We need to talk. I saw you get up, but I didn't want to scare you. Talk to me, Ria, *please.* I didn't cheat on you. I love you too much to do something like that." His voice sounds tortured.

"Really, Jax? I have a picture that says otherwise. You made promises to me. You broke that promise. You wouldn't even answer your phone when I called. I called your parents and they said you went out with friends and got clothes from their place. You didn't even have the common decency to call me yourself. What did I do to deserve that? You sent your brother to get your clothes from here. No call, no explanation. *Nothing.* It's over Jax. I deserve better and I should have known it wouldn't last. It never does." I pause for a second. "Bye, Jax," I sob out.

I hit end on my phone and turn it off. I later turn my phone back on, so I can call Alexis at eight, I know it's only eight, but I have a client coming in at ten and there is no way. It's a Monday appointment and I am so sick.

She agrees to go take care of my client for me and tells me to get better. She said she would call and cancel what clients they couldn't handle on Tuesday for me.

I do nothing but sleep, rest, and cry for the remainder of the day. I wake up the next morning not much better, getting up only when I have to. The day drags by and I call the girls later in the afternoon to let them know I won't be in the next day either.

It's Thursday and I am starting to feel like I'm human again, still emotionally devastated about what all has happened. I turned my phone on last night and had about thirty missed calls from Jax, and Eva called once. I just can't right now. Maybe when I have a chance to digest what has gone down, then I will meet the calls head-on.

As I get ready for work, I happen to glance in the mirror and see my dragon. My eyes start misting again. I take my hand and run it up and down my side on top of it. This will always remind me of Jax. I shake it off and go to work, the day drags by. I tell the girls that Jax and I are no longer together and that I really don't want to talk about it right now. I get a hug from all of them, but they don't push me. We get done for the day, everybody helps to clean up and we lock it up. Pulling into my driveway, I see Mrs. Franks and just wave, going inside. She is just looking at me curiously. I talk to Sassy as soon as I go in. I let her out and feed her, doing some laundry that has piled up. It's only seven but I decide I am going to bed. I am just done in. I take my medicine with milk again. I've lost my appetite and not had but a cup of soup in the last couple of days. I fall asleep, waking up at four in the morning from another nightmare.

I get up and get something to drink. I just go to sit down and the doorbell rings.

Who the hell would ring it at four in the morning? I look through the peephole. I can't believe this.

I wrench open the door. "What do you want, Jax?" I ask as he pushes his way in. He grabs me up, takes me to the couch and sets me on his lap. I am fighting him the whole time. "What the hell, Jax? What are you doing? Have you lost your fucking mind?" I screech at him kicking and hitting him the best I can. He takes my hands and wraps them around my back.

"Listen, beautiful. I didn't mess around on you. I promise. I don't know what picture you think you saw but it wasn't me. I did go to my parents. I had something I had to do. I got sick when I stopped to pick something up at the shop. Next thing I knew, when I woke up, I was in Toby's spare bedroom. I went to call you and I couldn't find my phone. I had to get another one. Toby came in with my clothes, said you would be gone when I came to get the rest of my things. That you said it was over and to kick bricks." He is spitting all of this out desperately in a voice from lack of sleep.

"No, what he said when he came and got your clothes was that you sent him to come pick them up," I yell. He is shaking his head no.

"I didn't, honey," he states.

I am shaking my head. I don't want to hear this. It's making the hurt come in stabbing waves of fresh pain. It hits me in the gut over and over again. I'm a big old blubbering mess.

"You caused this. You did. You lied and cheated. You made such a big deal out of all of this *I don't share bullshit* and then, what do you do? The first chance, you do what you said you wouldn't tolerate. I want you to leave," I scream at him.

"What picture? Look, I love you, beautiful. More than you can know. I didn't cheat, you're my heart. I went to go buy your engagement ring. I wanted to ask you to marry me. I met with a jeweler. I had to stop and get a check from the safe. I'll go because I can't bear to see you in this much pain. Remember this though, we are not over. When you're ready to listen, you know where I am. I love you, Ria," he whispers in my ear. He kisses the side of my head. He sets me on the couch and leaves. I sit there for I don't know how long. I hear him talking to Mrs. Franks. I get up and look as he gets in his truck to leave. I hear Sassy barking and scratching louder than ever before out back. I open the door and let her in, she runs to the front door barking.

"I know, baby, I miss him too, but I can't live with a lie. He hurt me too much." I groan in misery.

I lock the door, decide to just go shower and get ready for work.

I head into work early and get some of the weekly paperwork done, as well as the inventory order. At nine the doors open, and I start with my first two customers. I don't feel that happiness I normally feel when I cut a new style on a head of hair. This time though, it's like all the color has been washed away down the sink. The day progresses and before I know it, my last customer for the day is done and gone, I lock the doors and clean up.

Deciding I need some things from the store I head out, having this feeling that someone is watching me again. I park at *Walmart* and look around. I don't see anyone that is paying that close of attention to me, so I head inside. I grab a cart and get a few things for the week. I turn down the aisle by the cereal and glance up and my chest tightens and the breath in my body seizes. He's back. Hedrick is back. He looks me square in the eyes and there is no expression whatsoever in his. I grab my cart and go the other way. I go directly to check out, thinking *I need to call Trent.*

I gather my stuff and walk next to someone I don't know, all the while looking around to see if Hedrick is following me. I load the car and go as fast as I can, getting home in half the time. I grab my few groceries from the seat next to me, looking around before getting out of my vehicle. I lock it up, taking my keys in my hand like I was taught to defend myself. I have my house key in the other, unlocking my door as fast as I possibly can.

Sassy is yapping and running around, acting all kinds of crazy. I have no idea of what to do at this point. My nerves are stretched thin, feeling like they're going to snap any second now, and all of my emotions are at the surface. My lips tremble and I let out a small sob. I pick up my phone to call my savior again. There isn't an answer and I leave a message. I think of calling my mom but don't want to worry her and Daddy. I take a deep breath and count, just like I was taught in therapy. I sit down, trying to think of happy times. The longer I do this, the calmer I become. I can do this, hearing words from the counseling sessions, *you can do this…*

I get up after calming down and take care of my things. My phone rings and thinking it's Trent, I again just answer. I should have known better.

"I miss you, Ria. When are we going to talk?" Jax asks me yet again.

"Why would I talk to you? I thought we had been over this already. I have the picture," I say in a despondent low voice. *God, I miss him so much.*

"Ria, beautiful, I don't know what picture you're talking about. I love you and haven't been with anyone. I am telling you the gods honest truth. I have a receipt showing where I was that night. I went to buy your engagement ring. I stopped next door for a beer with Zeke. He needed to talk to me about something important.

He left and I talked to the guy next to me. I went to the bathroom and when I got back, the fellow had bought me a beer. I drank it with him and left. I had to go by the shop and get a check from the business account so I could go to the bank and deposit it into my personal account to cover the check I wrote for the ring I bought Ria. I got so sick that night, I don't remember much of anything." He tells me all this and I can hear the tears in his voice.

"Jax, I don't know what to believe anymore. I know things are not adding up. This is a lot to take in. I need to think. Give me until tomorrow evening, I will let you know what I decide then," I say this with a heartrending sob. I just place my thumb on the end button of my cell.

I drop the cell on the counter and go open the back door for Sassy, and she goes out. My front doorbell rings. Shaking my head, I have no clue who it could be, but I go to answer it. It's a lady from one of the local florists. I have a bouquet of red roses and they are gorgeous. I thank her and go to set them on the counter to look at the card.

> *"I love you with my whole heart, Ria, because you are my heart! Please talk to me."*
> *Jax*

I put it down and run to the bathroom. My face is nothing but a mess. It is swollen from blubbering. I mop up my face and I hear Sassy just going absolutely nuts. I leave the bathroom and as I am walking down the hallway, I notice that I forgot and left the front door wide open. I shake my head, heading towards the backdoor. Sassy is raising nine kinds of hell back there, and she has been acting off since Jax left.

I'm thinking that something or someone is manipulating the both of us, and in some ways, it makes me think his brother is part of it. If that's the case, I don't know what I'm going to do. Yes, I do, I am going to cold cock him.

I go to open the back door and am whacked upside my head with what feels like a baseball bat. That's the last thing I remember as I crash to the floor with a thump.

CHAPTER FIFTEEN

TRENT'S POINT OF VIEW

I look down at my phone as I come out of church and see I have missed yet another call from Ria. I can't push Debbie to call her right now. She has had some breakthroughs with her counseling, and she needs this time. I see she has left a voicemail and as I make my way to the bar decide to listen to it before I call her back.

"Beer," I tell the prospect. This is one that may make it if he continues to show us that he has the ability to be our brother and show his loyalty. He has gone above and beyond anything we ask of him.

I lift the can to my mouth and while taking the first swig of it my phone rings. I look to see who is calling; it's Franks widow. I pick it up right away. She only calls me when something is wrong.

"What's up Josie?" I ask in a gruff voice.

"She and her fella had a falling out of some type. He went by there this morning. She hasn't shut her door, so I went to look and she's not there. That mutt of hers is having a fucking fit. I can't get it to stop yapping. Something is wrong, and you need to get your ass up here now, boy."

"Hold on, Josie." I disconnect and listen to my voicemail from Ria.

"He's in town, I saw him. He looked at me with dead eyes. I've had a feeling of someone watching me for a while now. I'm scared Trent. Hedrick is around. At first, I thought it was Toby, Jax's brother. Jax and I have parted ways, but I think someone is manipulating things between us for some reason. Call me when you get this."

"Fuck, fuck, fuck." I am irate, and my voice keeps getting louder when I yell for my pres. "Garr," I growl out outraged. "We've got a big problem. Our girl is missing again, someone got her. Josie just called me. I just listened to Ria's voicemail and she has seen Hedrick. I smell a rat, and to top it off, she and her man split. She thinks someone helped to manipulate that too." I am fuming, and it all came out in a low deep grizzly voice.

"Let's load 'em up and head out then. We need to go hunting. Call Josie and let her know we are on our way," Garr tells me in a livid toned voice.

I call Josie back and let her know we are on our way and to keep an eye on the house.

We arrive within an hour and a half, pulling up to the house. There are twenty of us. Most of the men were at the clubhouse when the call came in.

Josie is running out of her doors as fast as her little ole legs will let her. A few years back, I had her move in here, so she could keep an eye on our girl. She keeps all of us entertained and has been good at keeping an unobserved eye on Ria without her knowing.

"I kept watch Trent, nothing in or out. That dog is having a fit," she gasps out.

I head into the house with just Garr behind me. The others are looking around and I hear a few motorcycles start up and head around the block looking for clues. I notice as soon as I open the door, the coffee cup sitting on the counter by the couch. I head toward the back. The bed hasn't been made, pajamas still on the bathroom floor. I come back toward the front and notice her phone on the counter in the kitchen. I pick it up and see my missed call. I unlock it and go through it; I see a couple of things I don't like at all. This is all wrong. She was taken against her will. She would never leave this stuff out and especially not with the door open. I let in Sassy and she sniffs my boots and sits on them and whimpers. I lean down and pick her up and rub the top of her head. I will need to come and get her later or stay here.

I look at Garr, and he looks at me with his brow raised, as pissed off as me. I glance down, thinking to myself about what needs to be done and notice that by the back door on the floor is a bit of blood or what looks like blood. I go over and squat down and look at it. It's not paint, that's for damn sure. Someone has taken my sister and whoever it is, they are dead.

I call Pete and let him know what's going on. We start to round everyone up, so we can decide who is doing what. The guys meet back here, and they let me know they found one set of footprints, probably a heavier male. We decide to split up, but not knowing what we're looking for, I have no idea other than we know Hedrick is back in town. I need to find that little fucker and have a long talk with him, using my fists if necessary. First things first though. I take Ria's spare key; a few of us will be staying until we find her. We get on the bikes and leave, making a straight line to someone who should have been taking care of his woman.

We all pull up in a line of rumbling mass confusion. I know they heard us coming down the block. I see Pete and the sheriff heading our way and nod my head at both of them. I know that the sheriff is as honest as they come, but he knows we can locate her before anyone.

I back my bike up to the curb and the others follow suit, with all of us dismounting at the same time. To some it may look rehearsed, but this is our brotherhood and we all just know what the other might do. This girl with long black hair is in the window looking out. She has a look of amusement on her face for some reason. She doesn't look scared in the least. We all step up and head toward the door. *Ink-Fusion* is marked on the sign above and has a great design on it. I've heard really good things about this shop and we at one time entertained coming up here for our tattoos. I am the first to stroll in. I look at the lady that was looking out the window and ask to speak with Jax and Toby just as they both walk out of the back. Two others peek out to see who is here. I just stand and glare at all of them.

The two come to a halt in front of us and Jax looks and speaks first.

"What can I do for you guys?" he growls out. He looks like he's pissed off and he has no idea his shit day is going to get worse. He looks like he hasn't slept in a week.

"Yeah, what were you doing at Ria's house this morning?" I ask him.

"Ria is my woman. We live together. Why do you ask and who the hell are you?" he growls at me.

"Well, I don't believe some of what you're telling me. Why did she fucking kick you out?" I smirk.

"Where the hell are you getting your information?" he says in an infuriated voice. "I want to know who the hell you are or get out of my shop," Jax spits out.

"My name is Trent. That's who I am, ring a bell with you?" I ask with an evil smile.

Toby speaks up, with a look of distaste on his face. The little prick doesn't know who he is fucking with. "This is the guy that I had seen kissing Ria. I told you Jax, she did. What the fuck are you doing here? The cunt was fucking you behind my brother's back," he stupidly says. Man, this guy seems to be tweaking a little, his face has a little sweat on it, and he seems to be shaking some.

I reach across the counter and jerk him up and over it with him landing on his knees in front of me. I jerk him up by his shirt, shaking him like a fucking rag doll. "Is that why you took a picture and sent it to her phone from yours?" I growl out.

"What the fuck have you done, Toby?" screams Jax with a voice filled with infuriated malice.

I pick up Ria's phone and show him the picture along with the other one. Jax takes his fist and cold cocks his own brother. Blood starts spurting out of Toby's nose and it's going everywhere. Commotion is everywhere. Someone had called Jax's parents and they come running in.

Jax is swearing and pacing around the reception area of his business, and it looks like the chick with black hair is trying to empty out the place of customers.

At this point I need answers, so I holler out at everyone and tell them all to shut the fuck up.

"I need answers Jax," I say as loud as I can at this point.

"Answers about what?" he says with a strong outraged voice.

"What did you two talk about this morning? Did she say if she had any plans? What was she wearing?" I growl.

"Why are you asking me these questions? Ask her," Jax mumbles.

Toby is muttering to his parents about what a cunt Ria is, sobbing and telling them that she is no good for Jax. That she ruined her best friend, Debbie. Garr is behind me growling now. I am done with this shit. I walk over and nail the little prick in the face again. More blood falls and it makes me smile a little inside. "Look you little fucker. You don't get to call my sister a cunt. As for my other sister, Debbie, you caused and imagined those problems, not Ria." I am so fucking pissed that I punch the fucker again. He goes down and he's out.

I turn to Jax. "Look, asshole, Ria is missing. I need to know what you know, so I can find her. Now quit being a fucking pussy and tell me what I want to know. I can't believe you didn't know what was going on with your own fucking brother and what he was doing to her. You don't deserve her." By the time I am done with saying all of this, Jax is in my face and I am in his.

"That's my woman, make no mistake about that. We had decided that there were problems from within and we were going to talk about it tomorrow night. Those were the plans. How do you know she's missing? What the fuck is going on, and I want fucking answers now motherfucker," roars Jax.

Garr steps in between us, telling us this isn't helping the situation and we need to get done cause each minute we argue is a minute more she is missing. Things start to settle down after that. I hear dinging on my phone. I am getting messages from Ria. Thinking that, that's not possible, I look down and see that it is. I look at Ria's phone and see where she sent a couple late yesterday. It's Hedrick. That is the only thing that makes any sense.

"Sir, I would suggest you get some help for your son. He is starting to tweak, and he's going to go through some tough withdrawals soon. He needs help. When he gets clean, I am whipping his ass again for pulling this shit," I let them know. No one hurts my sister.

Jax looks at his brother for the first time. I think he realizes what's going on with him. The other staff workers hear this and are nodding. Apparently, he is the only one not to notice, or maybe he has his head buried in the sand.

"I need to help you find her. I love that woman. She's mine," he chokes out.

"Dad, Mom, take him to rehab, now, get him the help he needs. He isn't allowed in the building until I know he's clean and in counseling. Until then, he has no job with me." Sounding defeated he tells his parents this. "I just pray that Ria is okay, and she listens to me. Dear God, what has happened?" Jax says in a muted roar. He grabs his keys and is right behind us. We have no clue of what is going on and I make a call to Whiz to find out if he found anything. He tells us he is getting close to Ria's. That is where he is set up to do more research and find Ria before something more happens to her.

We all mount up and go straight to Ria's. We glide in and dismount, all of us tromping into the house. Jax starts going through the house looking for Ria, he is extremely upset.

"Hey, Whiz, got anything yet?" I ask him.

"Yeah, just finishing up with what I've found so far," he replies. "I spliced into the city surveillance system, accessed a facial recognition application and got a hit. We are looking for a dark colored van. It's a two thousand four model. She was out cold it looked like. She was seat belted in the front seat. Doesn't make any sense. Whoever did this made it look like she went willingly.

Her head was tilted to the side and look here." He shows a picture he has blown up. *Blood.*

"I didn't get a good picture of the driver, but this is it." I look closer, and I recognize him immediately.

"I should have killed him when I had the chance," I roar.

"Who the fuck is that Trent?" Garr snaps.

Just about the same time, Jax speaks up and says, "Hey, that's the guy who bought me a drink that night in the bar. It's when shit went to hell with Ria. I still don't remember how I ended up so sick and passed out in my brother's bed," he says with bewilderment in his voice.

"Well, that's Hedrick. The guy Ria dated about three years ago. He was the one that had become verbally and physically abusive toward her," I tell both of them. I am so fucking mad at myself. I pick up my drink and throw it across the room. They all duck, and I scream out, "Fuck!"

"These are some properties that are cross-referenced with him one way or another. This here is his parent's address and this is his grandparent's." Whiz passes the papers to me. We are all looking at them when Jax leans over and skims the pages with me.

"Jax, this is going to get messy; you may not want any part of it. We will find her and bring her back to you," I state as I turn and look at the expression on his face when I tell him this.

"I don't give a fuck, I'm going. That's my woman and I let her down once. It's not happening again. You don't understand, Trent. She's my world, my heart. It doesn't beat without her," he says with a catch in his voice.

I nod my head. "Okay. Remember I warned you," I state empathetically.

We all take a piece of property, but we send two guys to watch the grandparents while we first hit up the parent's home. Jax comes with Garr and me.

We pull up outside the parent's home, located in a middle-income area. It's a brick home with black shutters. I notice someone looking out the front window and nod to Garr. He noticed too. We walk up to the door with Jax following and knock loudly with our fists. We wait and wait; I beat on the door again. I look at Garr and I head to the back of the house as he stands, upfront on the sidewalk waiting for me to give the word.

I get to the back; I look in the window and notice a man standing in a corner like he's trying to hide. *Fucking idiot. You want to hide, do it so no one can see you, dirtbag,* I think to myself.

I rear back and kick the backdoor in. He screams like a little pussy, and I cold cock the little bastard. He is out for the count. I shake my head as I start to search the house. I walk by and open the front door.

Garr and Jax walk in as I hear a noise from the hallway. I look at them and head down the hallway. I bust open all the doors, and at the last one I hear a sob. I head in and see a young girl tied up to the bed and she has tears running down her face.

Motherfucker. That's the only thing that comes to mind. I go forward, and she leans away shaking her head.

"Sweetheart, I am not going to hurt you. I'm going to remove this tape and it's going to hurt like a bitch," I tell her in a soft gruff voice.

I lean forward again, grab the side of the tape and rip it off as fast as I can. She screeches as I do this.

"What's your name and why are you tied up?" I ask.

"Tammy Sue is my name," I hear, as she sobs. "Please don't hurt me. I don't wanna be hurt again. Please, I just wanna go home," Tammy Sue says in a haunting voice.

"How long have you been here? Who took you?" I ask her.

"I've been here for a while; a man took me from a trail with my friend," she whispers.

"Where is your friend? How old are you?" I grumble out.

"I don't know where my friend is, I haven't seen her. I asked, but he won't tell me where she is. I'm fifteen," she chokes out.

"Get him to… fuck we have no place up here," I spit out.

"Yes, you do. I have a place out in the country a few miles. Four miles to be exact. I have a pole barn, no neighbors," Jax says, as he speaks up for the first time.

I make a call as Jax ties the fucker up. I call in Josie to come with the van. Tammy Sue needs medical help, so that means I have to call someone to help.

"We need some help with her and a medical doctor or a physician's assistant. Do you know any of those?" I say sarcastically to Jax.

"As a matter of fact, I have a customer who owes me a favor or two. He's a biker new to the area. They're setting up shop, or that's what they tell me. His name is Dog." He pauses for a minute looking through his phone. "He's with the Bitter Root Saints MC is what he said. Here's his number if you want me to call him."

"Garr? What do you think? We can't call in Pete, not at this time, anyway." Garr already has his phone to his ear and making a call to Whiz. He has him to do a fast search on this new club and anyone by the name of Dog affiliated with them. He also tells them we need that van and Josie asap. I look at Jax and it looks like he is ready to blow.

"You need to calm down. I know it feels like it's taking forever but this is a process of elimination. This first stop is a great lead. We just have to get all set up before we can get the information we need. He starts screaming here, we would have the local cops and who knows who else show up and we don't need that on us or on Pete. Understand me?

Jax nods his head. He has a look of livid furious intent of bodily harm, on whoever gets in his way of finding his woman. He loves Ria. I have no doubt about it.

"While we wait, tell me what the fuck happened with Ria. One day she is happy and the next you're out of her life?" I growl out in a seriously pissed-off voice.

"Man, you gotta know, I love her with everything that I am. I left work that day, one of my guys needed to talk to me about something important. I told him I had an appointment at the jewelry store. I had spilled ink on my shirt, so I stopped at my mom's to get a clean shirt." Jax sounds desperate, I believe what he is telling me. "Mom knew where I was going and promised to keep the secret, so when Ria called her, she just told her I had plans to go out with a friend. I left and went and bought an engagement ring for Ria. I went just down the block, went in and talked with Zeke. I went to go to the bathroom and when I came out the fellow that was sitting by my seat while I talked with Zeke, had bought me a drink.

I left after to go to the shop to get a check so I could transfer some money. I just remember getting really sick and I woke up the middle of the next day upstairs in Toby's room. Toby had my clothes from the house. He said that Ria didn't want me back, that she called wanting me to get my things. It was that guy Hedrick at the bar. He fucking drugged me," he spits out with an agonizing infuriating tone of voice.

"Sounds like it. So how long has your brother had a drug problem?" I ask Jax.

His eyes pop open really wide. "He never has, other than the occasional weed. That's always been his thing." Jax shakes his head, really at a loss, it appears.

"You know weed…" I start to say and stop for a moment to try to control what I say to him. It looks like he's suffering a shit ton at this moment. I continue, "That shit can get laced without his knowledge. You know who his supplier is?"

Jax is already shaking his head no. My phone rings just as the van pulls up. "Hello. Yeah, whatcha got for me?" I listen as I am told it's an affiliate club that we have done business with before. So, I hang up and let Garr know.

"Jax make the call. Tell Dog time is of the essence and if he can't help, we need to know now," I tell him.

Jax walks a couple steps away and makes the call. Dog apparently says he can help and Jax gives him the address to the country place, telling him we need medical attention for a female.

We load everyone up, the girl included. Josie road out with Jimbo in the van, and Jax is looking at us with a lot of confusion and, like what the fuck is she doing here.

I have mercy on Jax and fill him in, or some of it at this point. "Josie is an ol' lady to one of our past members. We lost Franks over twenty years ago. He was actually my sponsor. When Ria decided to move, I knew ahead of time, so I set Josie up in that house to help keep an eye on her. We knew that one kidnapper got away but didn't know who it was. It's a good thing. She knew something was wrong and called it in to us."

I can hear Josie talking to the girl. *Sounds like the same M.O. as when Ria and Debbie were taken years ago.*

"Did Ria know she was there to watch her?" Jax asks with more than a demanding voice.

He got a glare from me with a bellowed, "No!"

CHAPTER SIXTEEN

JAX'S POINT OF VIEW

We pull up and at this point I am madder than hell. Josie has been watching her for years and no one told her. She thought the old lady was just a great neighbor who needed company. I have no idea of what to think at this point. Ria had told me that Trent was her salvation after her kidnapping.

Sounds like he manipulated a lot of things. May be good, may not be either.

I get out of the van, and at this point I have no fucking clue where my bike went. *Fuck...* I think.

Dog comes out of the pole barn. I told him to pull in and get the doc set up in the cabin off to the side. I pray it's at least half dusted out. The cleaner normally cleans it out once a month. *Why the fuck I am worried about the fucking dust, I have no clue.*

"Dog," I say and shake his hand. "These here are some friends of mine. We have a situation that needs to be taken care of. Can you help me out?" At this point I am all kinds of pissed off. I go to the van and grab the fucker out myself. If he has any idea of where Ria is, I want to know and *now*. I am dragging that fucker in by his fucking arm and I stop and look, everyone is just standing there watching me like idiots.

"Well, are we doing this or are you all just gonna stand there with your hands in your fucking pants? This isn't finding my woman any faster, and I will not allow her to spend any longer with that fucker then humanly possible." I jerk my chin to the door as I continue to drag him out to the building. Trent comes up and picks up the other side as we haul his ass inside.

Garr looks at me with a mean bulldog look, I return it. I am tired of the run around, being left out of decisions.

I raise my brows; Dog asks what we need and before they can answer, I do. "Up on the engine hoist. Bring me a water hose that has been cut off. It's out on that other wall out there. Turn the overhead fan on to keep the noise level down, and we need a lookout." I just keep spitting out orders. Trent looks at me then Garr. I look at both of them. "Look, I will fight you all after, but time is a wasting. Let's get this shit done," I snap out enraged.

"I am going to kick your ass, son," Garr snaps.

I harrumph… with my lip in the air.

Trent chokes, and I smack him on his back and nearly knock him over.

He glares at me.

"Look, enough," I roar.

They have this piece of shit tied up and in the air by the time I get back there. I ask him his name, he laughs.

I pick up my stun gun, *The Runt,* it has one of the strongest milliamps at four-point-five. I ask him his name again.

"Fuck off," he says.

I light his neck up, hold it, and release. I ask again for his name.

"Fuck you," he mumbles.

"Dog pull his pants down," I tell him.

"His pants?"

"I didn't stutter," I growl.

He pulls it all down and I ask one last time for his name.

"Fuck you, you pussy," he groans agonizingly

I lean in and touch his groin with the stun gun and light that fucker up.

That asshat pisses all over my boot. I am so fucking mad I kick him in the nuts.

He is a blithering whiney mess.

"What's your fucking name?" I have lost my mind. I am so out of it I am shaking all over. "Tell me your fucking name or you ain't gonna have a dick left by the time I am done." I screech like a banshee.

"Derrick," he whispers out while retching.

"How do you know Hedrick?"

"Son," he gags.

"Where did he go with Ria?" I demand.

He doesn't answer. I pick up the stun gun and hit his dick with it. He vomits, head hanging down low. "Answer me motherfuck-er," I scream.

He mumbles, voice incoherent, we can't understand what he says, he's just a big blubbering mess. I look at Trent looking for a direction to go, Trent picks up Derrick's head and asks him where they are.

The man whispers, mumbles to Trent. I don't know what he told him, but Trent looks up at me and shakes his head. He releases the man's head, and we walk away.

"Did he say where?" I ask.

Trent says, "Out off of State Highway 425. Place out off the main road. He said coming toward twelve-ninety-nine going toward the college. You can't see the place, just an obscured driveway. We need to check in with Josie. Dog, can you take care of this fucking mess and meet up at Ria's when you get done?" Trent asks.

Garr is just staring at me. I stare back.

My phone rings. I look at the number, it's Ria's parent's number. "Have you told her parents she's missing?" I growl.

Trent shakes his head no.

"Do I need to pick up?" I ask. He shakes his head no. Now I feel like a piece of shit. Trent's phone rings next. He picks it up and mumbles. Its Ria's parents.

He answers it and I am so fucking mad at him.

"Hello, Dad. Before you ask, yes, I know she's gone and I'm already looking with Jax and the rest of the boys. We headed in early and have been working on it all day. I have a lead now. I can't stay on and answer questions right now. Whiz is at the house, he can update you." Trent sounds impatient with him.

"We are. Yes, I will let Jax know." He looks at me. "He said to bring his baby home." My eyes well up and I do my best to keep the tears from falling. I just nod my head. We all get into the van, minus the few that are cleaning up and the ones with the girl.

In all, there are six of us. Garr has rallied the troops and they are headed that way too. I need her to be safe and I need to know why? I pick up my phone and call Dog.

"Hey, it's Jax, need a favor man. Yeah, I know I owe you big. I want to know how long this has been going on. Get me all the information you can on these sick motherfuckers. They have been doing this for a while. See if you can get me names." I pause and notice the rest looking at me. I stare back. *I am not a fucking idiot.* "All the information you can get, make sure that little girl gets home, too." I nod my head listening to him. "Sure, deal," I say and hang up.

Trent looks at me. "What makes you think there are more?" he asks curiously.

"Too organized, too many places to hide. How many missing women in the last ten years in say a hundred-mile radius?" I state with a raised eyebrow. "Look, even if I'm wrong, it's better to get information while he's still alive. Did you know Hedrick had a dad? A grandfather?" I inquire. "We never did make it to the grandparents' place, now did we?" I state with a determined voice. I look at Trent. "Do you think she's there?" I say with an agitated tone.

"I'm not sure but we won't stop until we find her. I promise. She also has a secret weapon this time," Trent tells me.

"And that is?" I ask with a concerned look.

"She knows how to fight. She's a third-degree blackbelt. We taught her how to fight and fight dirty. She could kill a person with what we taught her. No one knows but the brothers. It was the only way to calm her fears. The condition was she couldn't tell anyone. That way if the fucker ever came back, he would be surprised and not know to expect it," he says gleefully.

I pray it doesn't backfire on her, I think to myself.

I need to find her. Make things right if I can. I want her to be okay. No, I need her to be okay. I don't pray often, but I am now.

As we come up on State Highways 1299 and 425, we see some of the guys on the side parked by some trees. I remind the guys that this is state boys' stomping grounds. I am assured that that is taken care of. Yep, out of the loop. That just pisses me off more.

Trent knows. He looks at me and shakes his head. "I will explain later. Not trying to keep things from you. You more than proved yourself earlier with the guys, and me."

I nod. That makes things a little easier to swallow. We all get out. We see Jimbo coming back out. I looked at Trent. "I thought he was back at the cabin?" I state bewildered.

"Old history, and he was the first one to leave. No way was he not going to be here. He was with me when we found her the first time. They have a bond, after being at the club for those three months. Easier to just let him come," Trent tells me.

"She's in there. She's tied up but didn't see much wrong with her. She looked a little more than pissed off. She made the comment that she dated the fucker and he was one of the originals to take her. She told him he was a sick motherfucker. I didn't know that girl could talk that nasty." He chortles with laughter.

"She's a smartass. It's one of the things I love about her. What are we waiting on? We got a sicko to go get. I want my woman," I say with determination.

"Hold up," Garr says.

I go to say something, and Trent grabs my arm to shut me up. I just look at him wanting to argue.

"Jax, you need to call Dog and see if he has any information for us. We may not have to get it from this, asshole," Garr states.

I dial Dog and put it on speaker phone, he tells me what he learned from the grandfather. "The grandfather learned from his father and so forth. Been going on for generations. Tells me the only time it was interrupted was when Ria was found. They use and abuse the girls before they sell them on the black market, or they sometimes kill them. He also tells me that the girl we rescued came from down by Nashville. Hedrick brought her as a peace offering for his dear old dad because of the last fuck up with Ria. Hedrick was forced to go into hiding for a while. The men couldn't take any chances around here and had left for over eight years. They had only been back a year, and they only came back because dear old grandpa has cancer and it's eating him alive." He says all of this without taking a break from talking.

"Anything else?" I ask sarcastically.

"Nah, that's bout it," he replies.

"Got it. Thanks, Dog."

We all take off and head in. We get about fifty yards from the door of the house, and we all hear a bunch of screaming, and rage coming from the house.

We all take off running, and I kick the door in. Ria has the fucker on the floor, and one of her hands is in his eyeball socket pulling the eyeball out. The guy is trying to roll away from Ria, but she isn't having any of it. She takes his eye and shoves it in his mouth. She has gone mad. Trent grabs my arm as I lurch forward to grab her. He won't let me.

"Watch..." he guffaws at me.

This isn't a laughing matter, but he thinks it is.

"Look, let her take care of this. It's good therapy for her. She will feel like she's in control of the situation." With a quick nod, I stand down and watch, ready to step in if I need too. Everyone is watching.

"You sick dirty motherfucking cunt. How dare you think I would want that shriveled up little fucking dick anywhere near me. Is that what it takes to get it up? Make girls terrified of you, you scum sucking prick? Huh, do you like sucking pricks, motherfucker, 'cause that is where you are going. They are going to treat you like their little princess. You damn fucking sleezy little measly mouth motherfucker. I am going to make you eat your own dick. You hear me you fucker. Swallow what's in your mouth now fucker." She takes the water bottle and pours it into his mouth. "Swallow it you little cunt." He does with fear in his eye. The guys all start clapping, and I can't believe what I am seeing. I never would have thought. "Huh... answer me you weak little fucking maggot. *Answer Me!*" She is screaming at this point. Her whole body vibrating with loathing hate. She has tears and snot running down her face, and if looks could kill, she would.

"I asked you a question fucker... Or are you that much of a pussy?" She is so determined to get an answer that she reaches forward and grabs his neck. She won't let him spit out anything remaining in his mouth.

"Swallow that fucking eye, you motherfucker," she screams with disgust.

My mouth has fallen open and I go to lean toward her but I am restrained again. They all shake their head no. My mouth is open in disbelief.

She is choking him. She releases him and goes to stand up. She turns and notices us all standing there. She looks at me. Tears running down her face and starts to come to me when all of a sudden, Hedrick jumps up and grabs her from behind. She goes ballistic, takes and reaches behind her and grabs his neck and flips him up and over. We all hear his neck pop. He lands on a chair that is broken and a piece of the wood lodges in his back and up through his chest. She stops and freezes on the spot. I reach forward and snatch her up in my arms. I take her out the front door and sit with her in my lap.

I croon to her as she sobs. "It's gonna be okay, beautiful, it's gonna be okay." I repeat this over and over. I get on the phone and call Dog to get out here. I tell him to make sure no one is watching what or where he is going.

CHAPTER SEVENTEEN

THREE MONTHS LATER - JAX'S POINT OF VIEW

Things are a mess for a while after we get Ria back. Once she calms down and takes stock of everything, she totally melts down. She has gone back into counseling for the time being. We are working on our relationship and she realizes what all has gone on. We are moving on with us though.

It's Saturday night and I got off work just a little early. I have the ring I bought three months ago. I plan on asking her to marry me tonight. I pull into the driveway and I see Trent's bike in the driveway, as well as a car I don't recognize. I shake my head, just praying that nothing bad is going on. My woman deserves good.

I walk in the back door and take off my boots as I go into the kitchen. There I see Trent and Pete with Pete's supervisor. Conversation stops when I step inside. Trent gets up and shakes my hand. "Brother," I say. "How have you all been?"

"Good, stopped by with these two. Grand jury said it was self-defense and any and all investigations are done. Pete's supervisor tells us all that it had been happening for years. At least two generations that they know of. They have found some of the girls taken. Some they found the remains of."

"Will you be in town for a little while, Trent?" I ask him.

"Actually, we will be. About twenty of us are staying out at the compound with Dog and his crew. Hope you both will come out for a cookout tomorrow?" he says.

I grin. "We've already been told to be there."

He smiles as they all get up. "See you tomorrow then." He goes over and gives Ria a big hug. "Love you, kid. See you tomorrow," he tells her.

I get up and walk them to the door, telling them all goodnight. I walk back in and Ria is taking dinner out of the oven. It smells good too. She sets lasagna on the table with a salad and homemade yeast rolls. She sets sweet tea and both plates. We eat and discuss how things are going at the salon since she's been back. She only went back a month ago.

"I'm glad you talked me into going back. No one has brought anything up and I like being back on my normal routine. Now if only Debbie would talk to me. I miss her. I miss my best friend. She sent me a letter with Trent. Says she loves me, but she needs to do whatever this is, on her own," I tell him with a sniffle.

We clean up and I walk up behind her, grab her around the waist, and start kissing her on her neck. I didn't know how much a person could mean to me until I met her. She turns in my arms and slips her arms around me. "I love you, you know that, right?" I tell her.

"I know. I love you too. More than you could ever imagine," she tells me with a big bright smile on her face. I get down on the kitchen floor and bring the ring out. "Marry me. Be my wife, and I promise to love you for the rest of our lives."

She is nodding her head yes, with tears running down her face and the biggest silliest grin ever.

I lean down and put the ring on her finger. She stares at it for a long time, twisting and turning her hand under the light to see all the sparkles. It's a one-and-a-half carat princess cut diamond. I pick her up and take her upstairs to get ready for bed.

We are in the shower and she goes down to her knees. She is running her hands up and down my body and each sweep gets closer to my dick. She needs to get there soon before I take over. I grip her hair and lead her face to where I want her. She runs her tongue up and down my shaft. She leans in and swallows me whole all the way to the back of her throat. I am in heaven when she does this. She has very little gag reflex, so I can pound into her mouth as fast as I want. She reaches down and slides her hand between her legs.

"No, that's my pleasure to give. I want that cunt tonight, all for myself." It's mine. She looks at me with a pout on her face. I just smile at her. She takes her fingers and plays with my balls, moving her mouth up and down my shaft. She has it lubricated from her mouth. She slowly and gently runs her teeth against the skin of my dick, and I erupt into her mouth. No warning, just there. I shove my dick all the way in her mouth for her to swallow my load. She eases off and makes a popping sound when she releases my dick. Still on her knees, she gazes at me with total devotion.

I lean down, hands under her arms and sweep her up. My dick is still hard and always is around her. I back her up against the shower wall, align my cock to her pussy, and in it goes. It's like a homing device, always knows where it belongs. I start moving with slow small soothing strokes in and out of her pussy. God, she is so fucking tight, and always clamps down on my dick. She is mewling as I lean in and catch her mouth. I pick up some speed going in and out of that juicy cunt. I can feel her clasp, tighter and tighter with each thrust. I am almost there again, and I know she is too. She was all primed for me while she was giving me a blowjob. She loves giving me oral but isn't much on receiving. I want to change that. I love her taste, sweet creamy peaches. She breaks from my mouth screaming through her climax as I attach my mouth to her neck and bite down.

As we come down off of our sexual high, she removes her legs from around my waist and slides down to the shower floor.

"I love you, Jax, more than you could possibly know," she says with the deepest feeling coming from her mouth.

"I love you too, beautiful, from the bottom of my soul."

I turn off the shower and hand her a towel as I start drying myself off. She does the same. I walk to the bedroom and Ria isn't far behind. I already have the bed covers turned down. I slide in naked and I'm ready for her to be in my arms. She walks in with a tee shirt of mine that she wears almost every night.

She snuggles down, leans up with her hands on my chest and her chin resting on top of them. Something is on her mind and I have no idea what.

"Do you think Toby hates me?" she asks with a miserable look on her face.

I am already shaking my head no. "No, never. The drugs got into his system quick. I went and saw him at our parent's. I told him we were going to get married, and he needed to get whatever problems he had with it out of his system now. He told me he never did have problems with me and you, at first it was because he was just looking out for me, and I can't understand why he did the things he did. He is more embarrassed than anything. He told me that when you're ready, he wants to make amends. It's part of his therapy. He seems to be doing better and will be coming back to work next Tuesday," I tell her with a smile.

I understand her concern and I was too until I talked to Toby. He really does seem better. I am happy for him. Glad he's coming back. I have had to work extra-time with him gone. I think I may look for someone part-time to fill in but who will also be a backup. People do get sick.

"Jax, I need to say this, so we don't fight later." Whispering she tells me this. My eyebrows are doing their funky bullshit now with them raised up. "We can't get married until Debbie is better and she can be my maid of honor. I need my best friend to help celebrate this happy occasion with us. I love you with all that I am, but I need her too," she tells me with tears running down her cheeks.

One of these days she won't cry like this. It tears my gut up when she does this. I am wiping her tears away as fast as I can. I lean down and kiss her on her cheek and then hit her lips. I go to sleep a very satisfied man, in more ways than one.

CHAPTER EIGHTEEN

I am just leaving my salon when I get a call from Samantha. "Hey, Samantha, how are you doing?

"Okay, but we're swamped, and I have back-to-back clients until later tonight. All the guys do too. Can you come in and help man the front today? Jax asked me to call you," she tells me and she does sound wore out already.

"Sure, give me a little while, about thirty minutes. Need to stop and grab something to eat. Anyone want a Subway sandwich? That's where I'm going."

She says she'll call it in at Garden Mile. I head that direction. I go in and place my order and it looks like they may be working on the other one too.

"Is that for *Ink-fusions?*" I ask.

"Yes, ma'am," I'm told.

"Okay, that's mine then, as well," I reply.

I get my drink, go back and pay for all the sandwiches. I take my drink and bags out the door and I go to my Honda. I get in and get to the shop just a few minutes later.

"Chow time everyone, I will put this back in the lounge."

Zeke and the rest thank me for getting them food. They get damn hungry when they are busy and can't go out to get their lunch without stopping work progress. I grab my sandwich and take mine and go to the front. I start checking everyone in and who they are going too. I take my clipboard and go through the electronic supply list. Jax had shown me one day how they take inventory, so that I could help out on Saturdays. It should be fairly accurate, but when things calm down, I will double-check the supply room. I start preparing the ordering for *Ink-Fusions* for the next couple of weeks. I have been working for a couple of hours when Toby comes up to me unexpectedly and gives me a hug. He has tears in his eyes.

"Ria, I am so very sorry for everything. I know it's going to take time, but I want you to know I am proud to be your future brother-in-law. You make Jax the happiest I have ever seen. Thank you," he says in my ear.

I give him a hug back. "Thank you, Toby, that means a lot to me." I look over his shoulder and Jax is leaning with his body on the side of the wall in the hallway watching his brother. I give Jax the biggest smile.

The day continues on and things start to slow down. I look up as the bell above the door goes off, and in walks in Dog. He walks up but looks like he has something on his mind.

"Hey, beautiful, Jax around?" he asks me.

"Yeah, hold on for a minute," I tell him and go back to Jax's room. I knock and he tells me to come in.

"Hey, honey, Dog is out here and says he needs to talk to you for a minute," I say concerned.

He lifts his chin. "Be out in a minute, sweets." He's putting his tattoo gun down and had already started cleaning the guy's back.

I walk back out and tell Dog he will be out in a moment to see him. He nods and tells me thank you, distracted. I ask if he's okay, and he's nodding his head yes.

Jax's customer comes out and I ring him up, take his card, and run it. He smiles and makes another appointment for one month. Jax walks out of the back room and walks up front. He walks over to Dog; I overhear him tell Jax he wants a piercing. I am listening or trying to. I hear Jax explain he isn't qualified and if he wants one, he will have to let Samantha do it. *Do it?* What's so big about letting Samantha pierce. She is good, and piercing ears, tongues, and such is no big deal. He finally nods his head and looks back out the window. Jax smiles as he walks past, and he goes and gets Samantha. She comes out a few minutes later and tells Dog to follow her to the back room and is gone for about forty-five minutes when he comes out walking bull-legged, red-faced and he looks like he has a great big hard on. Ummmm, now I know what kind of piercing he wanted. I keep a straight face, the best I can. I snicker and can't stop. I am bent over laughing like a loon when Jax comes out, takes one look, and tells Dog he'll bill him. Dog shakes his head, leans over the counter and tells me I better not tell a soul. I laugh harder than I ever have. "Be hard not to, Dog." Jax smacks my ass and tells Dog he will take care of it.

He tries to storm out but looks more like a frog march instead. Jax shakes his head at me and tells me he's going to go clean up so we can go home.

"Home sounds good, honey. I love you," I tell him with a smile.

"Ditto, beautiful," he replies.

Samantha comes out of her back room about ten minutes later.

She walks up beside me, leans in and hisses loudly, "That's the biggest fucking dick I have ever had my hands on. The biggest I have ever seen. My God, Ria, it stayed hard the entire time I pierced him. I've seen nothing like it ever... *Evvvveerrrrr!*

Her face is filled with not only excitement but determination. *I see a story here,* I think to myself.

Look for Samantha and Dog's story coming soon.

ACKNOWLEDGMENTS

Where do I start?

Hubby – Thank you for always being my rock, for pushing and believing in me even when I didn't believe in myself. I love you to the moon and back. I have the best Hubby in the universe.

My kids – Although, you are all older, you have always believed in me even when we drove each other crazy. You all are the best. I love you more than ever. So very proud of all of you!!!

Grandbabies – You are not really old enough to understand now, but when you get older, know that I love you babies to the end of this earth.

My other kids and family that I have adopted throughout the years –You all have helped make me who I am today. I miss each and every one of you.

To some of my favorite authors – It's your words and watching what you do that helped me to decide to try this. If I should fail, I know at least I tried. Thank you all. I don't really want to name everyone. I don't have a long enough page for that. You all know who you are.

I need to acknowledge a few people that have been there since the first word was typed into this computer.

Vera Quinn – one that I consider a close friend. Thank you so very much for not only your encouragement but your belief that I could do this. You never let me give up on myself. You let me rattle on when I had questions. Thank you for blessing my life. You are what true friendship means.

Maggie Kern – that magical day that I got introduced to you through AJ and Ricco. You and Greg are a part of my family and although you are my editor, you and Greg are a part of my family. I love you guys. Just remember all my cute little replies on edits. Hugs.

Michele Thomas – I couldn't do this without you in my life. You are not only a great friend but a rocking PA… I love you lady!!!

To Michele's authors – Thank you for any and all help you have passed my way. You all rock.

My crew – AJ and Ricco Bland, Kamilla Miller, Arlyna and Reuben Fischer, Wendi Hunsicker, Edward and Sarah Gillespie, Dyana and Thomas Newton, Hannah Hossler, and last but not least Kimberly Beale and Momma.

My beta team – Thank you from the bottom of my heart. Sara Parr, Wendi Hunsicker, Jenn Allen, Tammie Smith, Melissa Filla, Arlyna Fischer.

Aunt Beckie and Uncle Erwin – You all have no idea of what you mean to me. You, Auntie, stepped up and in when I have needed you. No questions asked, you were there. You don't know what it means to me to know you are there for me. I love you guys so much. Thank you!!!

CONTACT OR FOLLOW ME:

Penny's Author Page:

https://www.facebook.com/pennyanglene/

Penny's Reader Group:

https://www.facebook.com/groups/687547065063779/

 facebook.com/penny.anglene.50

twitter.com/AAnglene

Made in USA - Kendallville, IN
1175805_9781701140325
10.06.2020 1253